AND HE
A-SMILIN'

BY
ROY BRIGHT

Cover Art by Barry Renshaw

ISBN-13: 979-8693550087

Based on the screenplay, 'Toying'
by
Roy Bright & Michael Garrett Harris

Thanks to:
Mike Harris, Louise Rhodes, and to my very dear friend Sarah
Needham.

1

West Babylon, Long Island, New York.
Monday 1st October 2012, 10:30pm.
Subdued yet determined feet hurried along the suburban sidewalk, their owners having moments earlier piled out of a large, dark SUV that had then cruised away to the bottom of the street. The five-man S.W.A.T team moved in single file, locked tight into each other's backs and almost touching, their weapons tucked firm into their shoulders and pointed at the ground as they travelled down America Avenue. They quickly passed houses adorned with jack o'lanterns and other spooky decorations, their owners having been over-eager for Hallowe'en with the displays having been set out early in anticipation of the festivities. Across the street, and standing under a streetlamp, a man had spied the police team and, with a sharp tug on his dog's lead, had stopped his four-legged friend from whatever bodily activity it was about to conduct, forcing the animal to follow him at high speed and away from the area but not really understanding why.

The team stopped and hunkered behind a hedge upon arriving at the target house. The leading team member whispered into his comms to report the fact. They then quickly moved up the winding path through the well-kept front garden and into their designated positions, stacking up on either side of the red front door of the pristine two-story house adorned with lattices and covered in vines. The leader then called "Ready" into his comms and awaited further instructions.

While Team One set themselves in position, Team Two – who had evacuated the van a minute earlier and further around the block – performed the same routine, stacking themselves around the rear door of the house. Then, with a glance around to check, their leader called "Ready" into his comms too.

On the opposite side of the street to the front of the house, black-suited sniper Gerry Taylor dropped into a prone position on the flat roof of a house that gave him an unobstructed view of the target building and the front team, or "element", as it was known. Hastily, he unfurled the rifles bipod and pulled the butt of the weapon into his shoulder while sighting through its optical lens.

On the roof of a house a block away from him and overlooking the rear of the building, Gerry's partner, Donny Carmichael, performed the same routine, settling himself into position quickly and locking his sights on the rear element and the back door.

Further away and down the street, in a large van parked directly behind the S.W.A.T. vehicle, Detective Sergeant Rosalynn 'Rosie' Hendricks stood with her gaze fixed on the monitors displaying the feed from each team member's helmet-mounted camera. Removing her black leather jacket, she looked at her partner, Larry Jackson, then took a deep breath and turned toward S.W.A.T. Commander Lieutenant Frank Phillips, who stood between two seated personnel busy studying their respective monitoring equipment. After a thoughtful pause, she gave him an innocuous nod.

Frank returned the gesture, then spoke into his Bluetooth communication device. "Teams, report in."

Sergeant Phil Barnes glanced at his entry team and received a nod each from the breach, assaulters, and rear-guard positions. "Front element in position," he whispered into his comms.

At the back of the house, Sergeant Andy Kaminski did the same with his team. Satisfied with their nods, he said, "Rear element in position," in the same hushed voice as Barnes.

Next it was the sniper units.

"High Ground One in position," Gerry whispered.

"High Ground Two in position," Donny added.

"Copy; all teams in position," Sergeant Phillips said from the Command Vehicle. "High Ground One and Two, confirm element beacons."

Both Gerry and Donny sighted down their thermal imaging scopes, clicking them on and aiming at the helmets of each element's team members, to see small strobe lights pulsing at the back of each solid white figure.

Within the Command Vehicle, the team checked the display screens to confirm the pulsing beacons.

"Beacons up," Gerry and Donny said, one after the other.

"Anything comes out of that building that ain't our guys, we'll know about it," Gerry added.

"Copy. Stand by," Phillips said. He turned to Rosie.

Gerry sniffed and blinked a couple times, then wiggled his nose. He clicked his comms unit onto the private channel used by the sniper team. "Jesus," he said, with another sniff, "shouldn't be suffering with allergies at this time of year."

Donny laughed. "Probably allergic to gettin' a round in – as always, ya stingy prick."

Gerry snorted in response. "Hey, fuck you. I think you'll find it's deffo your shout this time."

"You gotta be fuckin' shittin' me," Donny replied with mock anger, "I paid last time, you freakin' crook. It's definitely your turn."

"Ah, come on, brother. You owe me, remember. I took one for the team with that barmaid's friend. Y'know, the really big chick. So you owe me, you owe me *big time*, Carmichael."

Donny laughed. "Oh, that's how it is, huh? Friendship acts determining the round score! Asshole."

"Fuck you," Gerry said, laughing, and his breath billowed into the cold night air. He sniffed again and looked back down his thermal sight.

Inside the Command Vehicle, after a brief conversation with the operators flanking him, Lieutenant Phillips looked at Rosie. "All teams in position, beacons up, and we're ready to proceed."

Rosie glanced at Larry and offered her a tight-lipped smile. She turned back to Phillips and nodded, signifying that the Commander now had control of the operation.

"Entry teams, camera for suspects," Phillips said, turning back to the monitors.

Upon hearing the instruction, the first assault position of each element took out a fiber optic camera and accompanying hand-held monitor, and wormed the cable under their respective doors, gently

3

pushing them into the rooms beyond; the front being the hallway, and the back, the kitchen. Each camera relayed information to their own monitor screen and to the ones in the van.

"No sign of threat, looks clear," each operator said, then retracted their cables and stowed them back into their pouches on their webbing belts.

Sergeant Barnes glanced at his team. "Front element ready for breach."

"Rear element ready for breach," Sergeant Kaminski said immediately.

"Elements clear to proceed," Lieutenant Phillips confirmed.

With that, both teams carried out their procedures almost in unison.

"Try the door," Sergeant Barnes said to his breacher.

The lead team member reached to the door handle and turned it as quietly as he could. He looked back to Barnes and shook his head.

"Okay, bring up the ram."

The rear-guard member then moved along the line with the battering ram, and the front assaulter moved out of the way slightly to allow him space. Pulling the ram back, he was about to thrust forward with force – an action his opposite number at the back of the house was also about to undertake – when Gerry's voice in their comms brought them to an immediate halt.

"HOLD!" Gerry said, "Wait! What the fuck?"

"What? What is it, Taylor?" Rosie responded, her brow furrowed and her eyes searching the monitor screens.

Lieutenant Phillips eyed Rosie with a venomous glare, then quickly returned his gaze to the monitors in front of him. "Entry teams hold." He turned off his comms unit so the teams could not hear him address Rosie. "Detective Sergeant Hendricks, I and I alone communicate with my teams when this phase of the operation is underway. Are we cl—"

Rosie held up a hand to him, an action that further incensed the man. "Talk to me, Taylor – what's going on?" she said as she turned her attention back to the screens.

"I can see the guy, Hendricks."

Her eyes narrowed. "What?"

"This shouldn't be possible, but I can see the guy, I can see his thermal image in my scope through the fucking wall."

Rosie checked her monitor; an action replicated by the other occupants of the vehicle. "The fuck you talking about, Taylor?" She turned toward Phillips, who checked the monitor and then frowned back at her.

"What the hell is he going on about?" Larry said, leaning over to investigate the screen in front of Rosie. "There's no image here."

Lieutenant Phillips shrugged at Larry, shaking his head.

Rosie glanced at the two men, then turned back to the monitors. "Taylor, we don't see anything here—"

"Look, Hendricks," Gerry said, cutting her short, "I am telling you I can see the guy's thermal image through the wall, like he's on fucking fire or something. Are you not getting this?"

Rosie's frown deepened and she stared at Lieutenant Phillips again, who could only continue shaking his head, his mouth opening and closing soundlessly a couple of times.

"What's going on, Command?" Sergeant Barnes asked. "We're a loaded weapon here – we going or what? Over."

"Wait one!" Lieutenant Phillips commanded.

Donny flicked over to the private channel again. "Talk to me, Ger. What's goin' on, good buddy?"

"Donny, I am telling you I can see the fucker, sat down in a chair in his fucking living room."

"You're freaking me out, Ger. IR don't see through walls or windows."

"Don't you think I fucking know that, Donny? S'why I'm freaking out myself, but I'm telling you I can see him…"

Gerry's sentence was cut short and he went silent for a second.

"Ger. Ger, you there? Talk to me, man!" Donny said.

Again, Gerry spied through his sight the thermal image of what seemed to be a large man, sitting in a chair directly facing him. He took a deep breath and quickly switched back to the general channel as the man stood up and took a few steps forward, appearing to leave another figure sitting in the chair where he had been.

"Whoa, wait, wait – I've got two targets now. What the fuck? I have two tangos. I repeat, another tango was sat on top of the fucker and has got up and is moving toward the east wall."

Growing increasingly agitated, Rosie stared at the monitor again and then flicked her attention back to Larry, her mouth agape, eyes narrowed, brow furrowed. "What do you mean, Gerry? We got nothing here. Confirm, over?"

The frustration of Team One's leader, Sergeant Barnes, peaked. "What's happening, Command? You callin' it or what, over?"

"High Ground Two, you seein' this, over?" Gerry said. He followed the second figure toward the east wall while the first remained seated in the armchair.

"Nothing, I got nothing, High-Ground One. What are you seei—"

Donny's voice was cut off. What followed was a scream so loud and horrifying, it made all team members flinch and paw at the communications devices in their ears.

Quickly, Rosie glanced at Donny's monitor that had cut to static fuzz. "High Ground Two, we've lost your thermal. High Ground Two, respond, over?"

Lieutenant Philips stepped in with more vigor. "High Ground Two, report. High Ground Two, do you copy?"

Silence.

"High Ground One, can you see him, over?" Phillips continued.

Gerry trained his weapon on the position where Donny should have been. "I got nothing, Command," he said, his voice high-pitched and rattled. "Donny. DONNY! Talk to me, brother."

Butterflies fluttered in Gerry's stomach and a lump gripped his throat, causing him to swallow hard a couple of times. Although desperate to spy any sign of his partner, something forced him back into the moment, to his job. He swept his rifle back to the house, acutely aware of the need to keep his eye on the bizarre targets.

Then panic hit him. "I've lost one!" he shouted.

"What?" Rosie said, furiously checking the screens again, in the hope of seeing something – *anything* – that might explain what Gerry had been communicating. "What do you mean you've lost one? Gerry, we have nothing here in your monitor. NOTHING!"

For a few seconds Gerry struggled to speak; then he attempted to compose himself. "Err, the other guy by the east wall is gone, and the one who was sat down is now stood up and is just… standing there. What the fuck is going on here, Hendricks?"

From behind him, Gerry heard what sounded like feet landing on the ground. He turned around just in time to see a shadowy figure reach down to grab him.

Within the Command Vehicle, Gerry's screams caused the team to flinch yet again, their attention drawn to his monitor as the image rose into the air and then the camera appeared to tumble for almost ten seconds, with an accompanying sound of rushing wind. Then the image flicked to static and Gerry's comms went silent.

Wide-eyed and breathing heavily, Lieutenant Phillips turned toward Rosie and Larry. "What the fuck just happened?"

"Gerry? Gerry?" Rosie shouted into her comms. Her heart raced and her breathing became erratic. Her mind swam with fear, to a level that she had only felt on a few previous occasions, when a bust had gone bad or she knew something awful was about to happen. That fear had her in its icy grip. It ran all through her body. Her mouth was dry, and her eyes darted from monitor to monitor, then down to the floor and back; her ears strained in her desperation to pick up any sound of either Gerry or Donny.

"Donny! Donny, can you hear me? Gerry, talk to me. What's happening, over?" she said, her voice quivering.

The voice of an angry Sergeant Barnes cut through the mayhem within the Command Vehicle. "Command. What the fuck is going on? We can hear movement in the house. It sounds like there are more than two targets. We need to move now. I repeat, we need to move now, over!"

Rosie's mouth flapped open and closed. It was Larry's stern voice, screaming at Lieutenant Phillips, that jolted her out of her trance. "SEND THEM IN! SEND THEM IN NOW!

Phillips reacted in much the same way as Rosie, startling himself out of inactivity that was alien to him, as he had never let a situation get beyond his control in all his years as a S.W.A.T. Commander. He screamed into his comms, "Entry teams move in. Assume entry point hostile, weapons free." He immediately questioned himself within his own mind to whether he had just made the right call.

"No, wait," Rosie said, her eyes wide.

Larry grabbed her arm. "They're going in, Rosie. We need to take him now. This is getting out of control."

The team member holding the ram drew it back once again and swung it at the front door, just as his opposite number in the rear element did the same. Each door took a couple of strong shunts before the hinges exploded and they opened, then those team members took steps back as the first assaulter positions threw in flashbang grenades that exploded with massive concussive force. Immediately, the other team members at the front of the house piled through the doorway and into the hall while the rear element followed suit at their position, each member shouting "Police' and "Get down on the ground" to anyone that might have been present.

Within the Command Vehicle, the monitors displaying the team members' helmet-mounted cameras went black. Everybody who had been watching got to their feet in shock as unfocused gunfire from multiple weapons came through their comms units, quickly followed by the terrifying screams of the S.W.A.T. members. Then some of the helmet-mounted camera images came back online, white-hot with flashes from the gunfire that appeared to be directed randomly.

Rosie drew her gun and raced past Phillips, who called out after her, but she paid no heed and instead threw the door open and ran into the street, pursued by Larry, who called to her continually as he gave chase. She bolted ahead, the screams of the men still battering her ears through her earpiece, though the gunfire had now ceased. Her breath puffed into the cold night air, and her mind raced feverishly with all the possibilities of what she might be running into, headlong and blind, as the shrill cries of the team members filled her head. Undeterred, she pushed those thoughts from her mind – she hadn't time for them. The team members – her friends – were in terrible danger, and the only thing on her mind was to get to them. To save them. She had to save them.

She screamed as she reached the doorway and the bloody and mutilated body of a S.W.A.T. member launched through it toward her; she had to dart to one side to avoid being hit. She stopped dead in her tracks, eyes wide, eyebrows raised and mouth ajar as blood spattered into her face from the butchered torso as it hit the ground. She screamed again as someone grabbed her from behind and pushed her to the side of the door. She looked to the opposite side to see Larry with his back against the wall, breathing heavily, having caught up to her and adopted a holding position across from her.

"What the fuck. What the fuck," He repeated, over and over, unable to take his eyes off the bloody mess at the end of the path leading up to the house. He leaned against the doorway, his gun pointing at the ground and his legs trembling. He closed his eyes and took several deep breaths, desperate to compose himself, to remind himself of who he was and what he was doing there. After a few seconds, and with the screams within the house having subsided, he opened his eyes and glanced across to Rosie, who had followed his example and positioned herself in a professional manner for entry.

8

"Okay. Okay, look," he said, his voice trembling. Desperate to hide any indication of his fear to Rosie, he closed his eyes briefly and took another deep breath, then exhaled through pursed lips. "Okay. Okay. Listen, we're cops, yeah? If we are going in, we're doing this right."

She stared at him, her eyes wide and watering. She tried to speak, to say something but hadn't the words. In the many years she had been on the force, no bust had come close to this event and the terror that now gripped her. Her legs shook, as did both hands gripped tightly around her weapon that was pointed at the ground. Even though her bravado had pushed her out of the Command Vehicle and had made her race up the street, what she felt as she leaned against the side of the house, waiting to go through the most terrifying, darkened doorway she had ever seen, was so powerful, so potent, that she thought she might relieve herself right there at any moment. And even though the threat had no physical appearance, she could sense it flooding out of the doorway like an evil and macabre mist, blanketing the stairs, flowing into the garden and the rest of the neighborhood.

Seeing her in obvious physical distress, Larry did his best to offer her a reassuring smile, but he struggled as his own terror was also rising fast. He took another deep breath. "It'll be okay, Rosie, trust me. We go on three." He closed his eyes once more, then started to count as he opened them. He had barely gotten past "One" when an unseen force yanked him inside the house and his terrified screams trailed off as he was drawn further inside.

With a scream of horror and defiance, Rosie pushed herself away from the wall and stood dead center in the doorway, panting, her eyes searching the blackness. She tried to move, to put one foot in front of the other, but could not. Tears streamed down her face. Then, the same invisible force dragged her inside and now her own screams echoed throughout the house.

2

Saturday 13th October 2012, 09:47am.

Rosie's eyes flickered open as she awakened to a steady beep that had permeated her dream. During her deep sleep, the sound had pulsed within her mind, accentuating and stirring the visions, the last remnants of which had lingered: she had stood at the edge of a great lake, covered in mist, and a voice had called to her from the water. The ethereal image of sliding into the water and making her way to the sound had all but gone, lost within her mind with the intrusion of reality. As her eyes opened fully and her lips smacked together, a foul taste within her mouth arrived along with her other senses, making her grimace. She tried to sit up, but felt uncomfortable due to something wiry sticking out of the back of her hand. She glanced at it to see a tube trailing upward. She adjusted her position, attempting to lean on the elbow of the offending hand and push herself up with the other, to take in her surroundings as best she could, though her vision was still blurred. She tried to call out, but the rasping in her throat prevented anything more than a forced whisper, and she had to swallow to try again.

"Hello," she said, then let out a dry cough. "Is anybody there?"

No reply.

She looked around again as her vision returned a little more, allowing her to gain a better understanding of where she was.

It appeared to be a hospital room, and a private one. She couldn't be entirely sure, as the blurriness had not yet dissipated, and she couldn't make out much more than what appeared to be a table at the edge of her bed, but she seemed to be alone. Turning toward the main source of light caused her to squint further. *A window*, she thought, and then she tried to turn in the opposite direction, assuming that would be where the door must be. She was about to call out again when she felt something on her finger snag on the bed sheets and come off with a snap. At the same time, the machine beside her traded its steady, continual beep for a higher-pitched, unbroken tone. She pawed at the bedsheets to relocate the item that had come loose, but to no avail. A few moments later she heard footsteps outside the door.

"Oh, hey there," a softly-spoken female voice said. "You're awake."

Rosie shifted her position in an attempt to sit upright, but the effort locked her face into a mixture of discomfort and determination, and she huffed.

"How are you feeling, detective?"

"Where… where am I?" she asked, her voice still croaky and uncomfortable. She looked down at the bed as she attempted to clear her throat.

The woman took a couple of seconds to answer. "You're at Good Samaritan, Detective Hendricks. Umm, there's an officer outside. I'll let him know you are awake and have him call someone, okay? Umm, I won't be a minute, err… I'll be back in a second."

Rosie frowned at the obvious nervousness the nurse exuded. Her vision began to return sufficiently enough to see the woman with more clarity. She was a pretty, petite blonde with a welcoming smile, dressed in navy-blue scrubs. The ID badge pinned just under her left shoulder was too far away for Rosie to read.

"Yeah," Rosie said, wetting her mouth again and clearing her throat. She gave a quick glance to either side of the bed as she attempted to force herself closer to a sitting position. The nurse began to move away quickly, but Rosie stopped her before she walked out of the door. "Hey, how long have I been here?" she asked, grunting a little from the effort of trying to make herself comfortable.

The nurse looked around. Yet again, she seemed to be struggling to decide what to say, as though the information was not hers to give.

"How long?" Rosie repeated, this time more forcefully and accompanied with a penetrating stare.

"Two weeks, detective."

Rosie exhaled and her mouth hung open; her eyes wandered. After a few moments of abject confusion, she said, "Larry. My partner, Larry Jackson at West Babylon P.D. Can you call him, please?"

The nurse's demeanor became more agitated, her mouth opening and closing but making no sound. She fidgeted with her hands as her eyes darted around the room, as if not wanting to meet the patient's. She shook her head slightly. "Umm. I'll... I'll just get the officer," she said in a wavering voice, pointing out of the door and down the hall. Then she scurried away, leaving Rosie staring after her.

"Can I at least get this shit outta me?" Rosie shouted, her hand held aloft and the drip tube rising with it.

****

Rosie gazed out of the window from the armchair next to her bed, her attention fixed beyond the sky outside, into a different time and place, the last remnants of the lake dream now far away at the back of her mind. Her knees were pulled up to her chest, her chin resting upon them, the freedom of movement welcome after the removal of the drip and heart monitor along with all the other bodily intrusions. She'd been sitting like that for almost an hour, pondering vacantly, because no one would tell her anything. Not Dan Starrens, the uniformed officer who had been posted outside her door and who had entered the room briefly to chat but had then quickly returned to his post, stating procedure or some other shit; and certainly not her attending nurse, who had avoided answering any of her questions at all costs, resorting to her nervous smile and warm demeanor whenever Rosie had raised any questions. Not that Rosie didn't like these attempts at calming ways; she thought the woman was probably a terrific nurse, adept at making her patients feel at ease and comfortable – under normal circumstances. But these *weren't* normal circumstances, and Rosie wanted answers; lots of them. It was in her nature. It was how she functioned. And without answers, she felt worse than a third wheel: she felt useless, unable to come to terms with events that had directly affected her and ones that she was having severe difficulty remembering, never mind piece together.

She sighed, realizing she had to pee. She tried to stand, holding her stomach and wincing. The pain had been much worse when she had first made her way out of bed and into the armchair; but despite the nurse's protestations and calls for her to take it easy, she had waved the woman away, needing to do it herself, to prove she wasn't totally helpless. She might not get any answers when she asked for them, but she was damned if she was going to behave like an invalid, to hell with any medical advice. She knew her body better than anyone. Of course, she regretted her decision. The nurse had been right; it had been too soon to move as quickly as she had, and to such a degree after having woken from a coma. Rosie knew she should've listened. But she was who she was, and she hadn't. She shook her head as she crept toward the bathroom, inching along.

A coma, she thought. *A goddamn two-week coma.* She had done her best to remember the night of the bust, but had no recollection of anything after leaving the Command Vehicle. That bothered her a great deal, but no images presented themselves: zip, nada. A blank screen where sights and sounds normally ran rampant, full of meaning and potential answers. She closed her eyes again and grimaced, in part due to the pain, but also the rising anger that had been building within her. She was desperate for answers and, more so, for information about Larry. A horrid, dark feeling had been brewing in the pit of her stomach, a sensation that had always told her when bad things had happened or were about to happen. It was rarely wrong. The thought had made her feel sick to her stomach, as the obvious conclusion was unbearable to imagine.

At last, she made it to the bathroom and sat on the toilet, with much effort required to bend her knees and place her backside on the seat. She was grateful for the invalid rail to one side; something she had never imagined she would have to use at her age. But there she was, inching herself into position, utterly dependent on it.

Having finished weeing, she got up, washed her hands, and then examined herself in the mirror above the basin. Groans followed a deep frown "You look like hammered shit, Hendricks," she said with a shake of her head. Then she placed her thumb and forefinger on the dark rings under both eyes and pulled down to fully reveal the full extent of their bloodshot appearance. "You really, really look like hammered shit."

She turned slowly to one side, checking the cause of the pain on the right side of her neck. It was then she saw it. A bruise, deep purple in color, large and thumb-shaped. She winced as she moved her head to look at the other side and saw four more distinct bruises that could only be the deep indentations of fingers. Someone had grabbed her by the throat. She drew in air over her teeth, then dropped the hospital gown to the floor to examine her body, turning from side to side to peer over her shoulder and gaze into the mirror, an act made more difficult by the pain. Deep scratch marks tracked across her back in fours. She attempted to touch them, but sharply drew in breath as pain under her arm forced her to stop. Lifting her arm, she saw large, purple-blue marks just beneath and to the side of her breast and, upon examining the other side, the same marks there.

Her attention shifted to a knock at the door.

"Rosie. You in there?"

"Yeah. Just a second," she called back, recognizing the voice of her colleague, Detective Sergeant Paul Keenan.

She hurried as best she could to put her gown back on, desperate to talk to him. He was a cop with a long and successful career, and a friend she trusted implicitly. He had been her mentor upon joining the West Babylon P.D. homicide division about two years into her career. It had been his exceptional teachings and patient instruction that had seen her rise fast within the ranks to become Detective Sergeant herself in just two short years. She owed a lot to Paul and respected him even more so. She felt certain he would have the answers she had been seeking all morning.

After dressing, she opened the bathroom door and hobbled back to her room, a protective arm across her rib cage. She looked up at Paul and attempted to smile, but she suspected that the pain that racked her body made her look mental, so she gave up with a grunt.

Seeing her awkward entrance, Paul hurried from the bed and approached her, his hand outstretched to offer assistance, but she waved him away with yet another grunt.

"It's fine. I got it. I'm okay." She attempted the smile again, this time with a little more success, then moved to sit on the end of the bed.

He stared at her for a few moments with a wry smile, before moving to the armchair. "How ya feeling, kiddo?" he said.

"Like a two-week coma's worth of ass-kicking. Whaddaya think, Keenan?" she replied with a playful smirk.

He nodded and snorted laughter through his nose.

Her smile waned. "But… I'm feeling very much in the dark here, buddy. Been awake a couple of hours now, but no one will tell me squat."

He looked down at his fidgeting hands.

She took a moment to ponder her next question. She knew what the answer would be; she had sensed it all morning since getting out of bed, though she hadn't wanted to hear it. But she had to ask. She needed to know.

"Larry?" she asked, then looked down at her hands clasped in her lap before returning her gaze to him.

Paul looked up at her, and shook his head slowly. He pursed his lips, then reached out and patted her hand and offered a sympathetic smile.

She turned toward the window, trying to shield her face as her breathing begun to shudder and tears welled in her eyes. It was no use; the tears fell, and she knew Paul saw them before he respectfully allowed her some privacy and turned away.

Neither of them spoke for a long time.

Eventually, Paul broke the silence with a deep intake of breath. "What the hell happened, Rosie?" he said, his brow furrowed and his eyes narrowed. "It was a goddamn massacre. I've never seen anything like it before in my entire life."

She looked at him sharply. Her mouth hung open and she then shook her head. "I... I don't know, I really don't. But I have never felt anything like this. It's like there's a huge black hole in my mind surrounding anything to do with what happened after Larry and I left the Command Vehicle."

"Well, that's just it," he said, sitting forward in the chair, "that's all we have to go on from the buggy's internal cameras and comms. You and Larry high-tailed it outta there, and that's it. Nothing more. And things are escalating, Rosie. Answers are required. It's been enough time now for people to put their grieving on hold and to want briefing. They wanna know what went on in there, because nobody but you made it out. You sure you don't remember anything?"

She closed her eyes for a moment and said nothing, then her lips moved without producing any sound. Eventually, she exhaled and sagged. "Nothing much," she said with a shake of her head. "I remember Larry and I being in the buggy, then..." She looked down at the floor, distant once again. "Screaming. Lots and lots of screaming."

He frowned. "Screaming? You were screaming? Or Larry?"

She didn't answer, instead continuing to stare at the floor.

"Rosie?" he said, leaning forward.

"Huh?" she replied, looking back up at him sharply.

"You said 'screaming.' Who was screaming?"

She stared at him for a few seconds. "Everyone." Her eyes widened. "Everyone was screaming."

Paul's frown had deepened, and he sat back, mouth agape.

Rosie blinked, then shook her head. "I really don't know what went wrong. It should have been a cinch. Just one guy to take down—"

"Yeah, but one dangerous bastard, from what I understand."

"Sure. But we had the high ground, front and rear elements, the upper hand. Should have been just a quick breach and grab. Nothing too strenuous." She took a deep breath and narrowed her eyes. "I kinda remember running down the road, then stacking on the perp's door. I think. Did I do that?" She glanced at Paul.

He pursed his lips and shook his head, his eyebrows raised. Then he leaned forward again. "Rosie." He reached over and grabbed her hand, making her look at him. "We really need answers. You understand. We lost everyone. Everyone, Rosie. S.W.A.T., the buggy team, Larry, everyone. Everyone but you, that is, and all eyes are on you at the moment. So for your own sake, you really need to get back on track and your head in the game."

She exhaled a sharp laugh. "Don't you think I know that? You want an explanation. They want an explanation. Well, so do I." She took a deep breath. "I just need to sort my shit out, retrace my steps and get my bearings. I'm sure it'll all come back."

He stared at her for a few seconds then offered a faint smile and sat back in his chair.

"I wanna get this guy, Paul. I wanna nail this fucker."

He nodded. "We all do. And we will, Rosie, we will. But you need to rest now and heal up. Okay." He leaned forward once again and patted her hand. She smiled at him, and he sat back and crossed his legs. "We're gonna need to take your statement and debrief you to help get things moving from your perspective and have a starting point for the investigation."

She nodded, breathing sharply through her nose.

"I'll send someone over ASAP and get you started. Who knows, maybe it will all come flooding back when one of the guys runs you through it. Captain Banks wants you to get done soonest and get psych-eval'd before he can consider you for active duty."

Her attention snapped to him. "I don't need a psych-eval, yeah! I'm fine. I just need a few days, then I'll be good to go."

"Rosie. Don't even start with that shit. There's protocol and you know it. Ain't no one gonna let you go back into the field without one after what happened and all you went through, so please, just… don't. Besides, I.A. want a chat with you, also."

She took in a deep breath, her eyes widening. "Aww, fucking great. That's all I need."

Paul uncrossed his legs and sat forward again. "Hey, I'm your friend, with your best interests at heart, Rosie, but you know the drill. Internal Affairs are just doing their job, same as you and me."

She sighed, looking down at her hands and clasping them together.

"Like I said. A lot of people want to talk to you. We need to know what happened in that house, Rosie – 'cos I gotta tell ya, the way in which we found the team in there was fucked up. Fucked up beyond belief. And… well, yeah, we need to know." He stared for a few seconds then drew in a deep breath and stood up. "Look. Get yourself fit and, y'know, jump through the hoops, then come back to work, 'kay?"

She stopped fiddling with her hands and looked up, then smiled.

He smiled back. "At present, the case ain't going nowhere, and I mean that literally. The guys will need you on this one to help start putting it all back together, but you need to be right. So get some rest, Hendricks. That's an order… from Captain Banks, that is."

She nodded a little then attempted a salute, but only succeeded in aggravating her injuries again, making her wince, so she gave up.

"For fuck's sake, Rosie," Paul said with a chuckle as he walked out of the room.

3

Monday 22nd October 2012, 3:30pm.

Rosie struggled to remove her key from the lock, cursing as she wiggled it left and right, the brown bag of groceries held in her arm adding to her irritation. At last, she pulled the key out and shuffled into her apartment, bumping the door closed with her backside, her chin holding the bag stable.

She sighed and looked around, happy to be back home finally, then her nose wrinkled at the slightly stale odor of an unventilated apartment. She moved into the kitchen and plonked the groceries onto the counter, then dropped her backpack onto the floor and moved around the apartment, opening windows to circulate the air. In the living room she stopped to look around, then from the kitchen she retrieved three plug-in air freshener refills from the bag and moved back through the rooms to change out the units.

Next she began unpacking the rest of the groceries and laid them onto the counter, grouping foodstuffs together; her usual routine and methodical approach to storage. When she opened the fridge she screwed her nose up at the smell. "Goddammit," she said, then immediately set about removing spoiled items, including a swollen carton of milk which disgusted her most of all, as she had a real disdain for spoiled dairy. She tossed most of the items into the trash, then poured the rotten, coagulated dairy gunk into the sink with an "Uggh!" before washing it away and adding the container to the trash. She then reached under the unit and retrieved a pack of anti-bacterial wipes and got to work cleaning the fridge. After a few minutes, and satisfied she had done a good enough job, she resumed putting away the groceries, turned on the coffee machine, and emptied her backpack.

18

Ambling into the bathroom, she stuffed her dirty laundry into the hamper, undressed and jumped into the shower, happy to once again be able to use her own amenities and relishing the hot water splashing over her skin, her head resting against the wall just under the shower head.

Thankfully, she had begun to look better than she did when Paul had come to see her, the dark rings under her eyes having subsided considerably and the bruising settling to a muddy yellow, with only small spots of purple-blue within them. Not only that, she had felt infinitely better than the hours after she had woken from her coma – something for which she was grateful, as that had been the most uncomfortable pain she had ever experienced.

She lifted her head and allowed the rushing water to splash into her face, turning to her left and right as she did.

After about twenty minutes, she stepped out into the steam-filled room and wrapped a towel around herself. She wiped the fogged mirror and engaged in a race to study herself before the steam once again overwhelmed its surface. She sighed, took a small towel from the rack and wrapped it around her head, then moved into the kitchen and poured herself a very welcome cup of coffee: proper coffee, not the awful shit they had been serving in the hospital. She moved into the living room and set the cup down next to her laptop, then turned it on and sat in her computer desk chair as the machine played its start-up chime. She entered her password at the prompt and allowed the computer a few moments to fire up its desktop – which didn't take long – and then opened up a browser and began catching up on news and events, interspersed with drinking her coffee.

After a half hour, Rosie removed the towel from her head, having given her hair a final and vigorous rub, then mussed her hair and allowed it to drop. She made her way into the bedroom, got dressed in slacks and a T-shirt, then walked back into the living room, grabbed her mug, and went back to the kitchen for a refill. In the kitchen she stopped and frowned at the open fridge door. Did she forget to close it properly? She knew she was a little scatterbrained of late, her attention drifting from one moment to the next and not remembering what she had been doing; it was something her doctor had told her was completely normal following her ordeal. But she had been sure she had closed the fridge. She rolled her eyes as she closed the door again, refilled her mug from the jug on the percolator, then made her way back to the table and sat down before her laptop. She grabbed a notepad and a pen and started to make notes.

Forty minutes later, Rosie threw the pen down and grunted, then rubbed her forehead with the palm of her hand. She had been getting nowhere – most of the time had been spent staring at the laptop screensaver as her mind drifted further away from what she had wanted to concentrate on: the events of that fateful night. But try as she might, she couldn't seem to get any scenes to play out, other than what was locked inside her mind already (and that hadn't been a great deal). She had closed her eyes tight, attempting to will the memories back into her mind's eye, to try to force something through – anything that would give her fresh information and lead her down a new path and toward answers. But it was no use. She glanced at the pad; all that was written was:

– *SWAT headcams*
– *Solid visual*
– *Shots and screams from inside*
– *Me and Larry at the door*
– *Then......?????*

She held the notepad to her forehead and pushed hard, her eyes closed.

Nothing.

Worth a try, she thought, then threw the pad onto the table with a huff. Standing up, she grabbed her mug and returned to the kitchen, then came to an abrupt halt. She glanced around the room and then back into the kitchen. The fridge door was open... again.

"For fuck's sake," she said, stomping toward it and placing her mug on the counter. "That's all I need, a fucking busted fridge."

She closed and opened the door a few times and was surprised to find that the seal magnets seemed to be in working order. But she didn't want to chance her newly-bought provisions going off, so she rifled through one of the kitchen drawers to find a roll of duct tape. She cut off a couple of strips and placed them at the top and bottom of the closed fridge door and around the side, holding it in place.

"Right. Stay there, you!" she said with a determined nod of her head.

She would ring Paul later, she thought, and see if he knew of anyone who could come and look at the fridge. She didn't want to have to buy a new unit, as this one had cost her a fortune due to the odd space that the landlord had deemed fit for the appliance, nor did she have the cash to drop on a replacement. Eyeing the fridge one final time, she pushed against its door just to make sure, then had started to walk back to her laptop when she remembered what she had come into the kitchen for in the first place: more coffee.

****

Watching, as Rosie whirled around with an annoyed grunt, a dark and shadowy presence stood in the hallway that led to her bedroom.

4

Wednesday 31ˢᵗ October 2012, 8:00am.

Rosie puffed and panted hard. Her pace on the rowing machine was incredibly intense. She had always been in great shape her whole life, but for the last few days something inside her had told her she needed to be fitter, stronger. That had also been due in no small part to her aggressive desire to get back to work at the precinct as soon as possible. She wanted to nail the guy, the individual who had committed the horrific acts and changed her life forever. No, she *needed* to, so that she might at last get some answers and finally move toward some sort of closure over Larry's death.

His passing had hit her extremely hard. Not only had he been the best partner that she had ever had, they had been close; too close to allow anyone at work to know about. They had kept their romance under wraps – not that there had been anything sordid about it. They had both been single, with no significant others to hurt, but departmental policy forbade officers from forming sexual relations with one another. If the truth had gotten out, one of them would surely have been transferred – and not seeing Larry every day was something Rosie hadn't been willing to risk. But no matter how careful they had been, how close to their chests they had played their cards, in the end the job had had the final say and she had lost him. And it had hurt.

As Rosie pondered that fact and the pain began to grow, she put even more effort into her rowing strokes, increasing the pressure on her already over-capacitated lungs. But she wouldn't stop. She would never quit. She couldn't. It wasn't her way. So she gritted her teeth and saw out the last 250 meters in just over a minute; her face reddened, her knuckles white and her lungs fit to burst.

At last, her 6000 meters was up, and she let go of the handle, allowing the chain to retract to the edge of the cage surrounding the wind-resistance wheel with a clatter. She bent over, gently rocking the seat back and forth on its track, attempting to get her labored breathing under control. After a few minutes, she stood and walked to the weights section and took the desired ones from their rack.

A young man approached her. He was probably in his mid-twenties and was someone she recognized enough to say 'hi' to at the gym. He was in great physical shape, and it was clear he knew it, and liked it: Rosie had noticed him admiring himself in the mirror on many occasions.

He held up a hand as he approached. "Hey. You're back. Haven't seen you around for a while."

Rosie smiled and grunted as she lifted a set of 46lb weights from the rack and moved to an exercise bench with its back already set straight up. "Ah well, y'know, I've not been so good lately, so I kinda took a break." She sat down and placed the dumbbells on her knees.

The young man pressed his lips together and nodded, scratching behind one ear.

She smiled again, then lifted the weights above her head and began her shoulder press routine.

"Wow!" he said, raising his eyebrows. "Pretty strong for a girl."

Rosie stopped with the weights above her head and looked at him for a moment, her eyebrows raised a little.

The young man grew even more awkward and forced a smile. "Yeah, well. Good to have you back. I'll leave ya to it. See ya." He smiled again.

"Yeah. See ya," Rosie replied, not bothering to smile back at him, and then continued her workout.

****

Dr. Mary Williams sat in a red leather chesterfield seat, her legs crossed with a pad on one knee, and her fingers steepled under her chin. She stared at Rosie for a few seconds, saying nothing, just observing the detective as Rosie glanced around her office that was extremely neat and minimalistic save for three large bookcases affixed to the walls, each filled to the brim. Between them was a small, oval coffee table, and on it, close to Dr. Williams, was a file labeled with Rosie's name and rank information. At Rosie's end of the table was a steaming cup of coffee made for her by Mary; something she insisted on doing herself – despite having an assistant – as a matter of courtesy to create an air and sense of calm before discussing the matters at hand. This was especially important as members of law enforcement formed the majority of her clientele; her being the sanctioned precinct psychiatrist. These people could be wound tight even before a single word had been uttered.

Most of Dr. Williams' clients had an innate and deep mistrust of 'shrinks', since in many cases they were the last obstacle to overcome before they were allowed back into the field. True, many of her clients came to her in times of need, as people did with all mental health professionals, but in Mary's case, most were post-traumatic cases. Usually this involved shootings, done by or to her clients, and in almost every instance, a certain amount of hostility came with each session. Human emotions are a complex thing, and cops having to explain their actions in a job that was difficult and involved split-second life or death decisions, even more so. Therefore, Mary's way was to make them a drink and start off on the best footing she could. So it had been for the fifteen years she had served the West Babylon P.D. and other precincts. And she was very well respected. Her success rate at getting officers back into work, or off the streets, depending on the circumstances, had been immense, and with that came much acclaim.

But as Mary sat across from Detective Sergeant Hendricks, watching her reach down to take her coffee and drink from it, she felt that something more was afoot, something she just couldn't put her finger on. From the brief conversation she had had with the officer –nothing more than pleasantries as she made the coffee – she had sensed a calm in the woman that perplexed her. Most officers who came into her office for psych-eval, and who had a desperate need to return to work, were jittery, eager to please and to show how ready they were, but not Hendricks. And Mary hadn't yet figured out if this was the measure of the woman, or if she had deep and long-lasting trauma that would mean she would not be able to pass her fit for duty.

Mary breathed out deep, through her fingers, then dropped her hands to her lap.

"So, Detective Sergeant Hendricks—"

"Rosie," the detective said, interrupting her. "Just… Rosie is fine. No need for formalities, doc." Rosie then huffed a laugh and closed her eyes briefly. "Yeah, I'm aware of the irony."

Mary offered a small smile. "Very well, then. Rosie it is. Feel free to call me Mary if you like."

Rosie smiled. "I think I'd rather call you doc. Feels… right. Y'know?"

Mary smiled again. "Whatever works for you, Rosie." She took in another deep breath and studied her pad. "So. What exactly do you remember?"

Rosie pursed her lips and shook her head. "It's all there in my report, doc," she pointed to the file in front of Mary. "Everything I remember."

Mary studied her for a moment, then breathed out through her nose. "You know, sometimes when deep, psychological trauma happens due to something horrific, we try to bury those feelings and associated emotions deep within ourselves as a defense mechanism, and that can lead to memory loss. Usually this is temporary, but its exact duration can be dependent on the individual. What does seem to help, in my humble opinion," she reinforced the point with a gentle smile and a hand placed on her chest, "is talking it through, no matter how sketchy the facts may be. Discussing such things in a comfortable and controlled setting has led to many a breakthrough in my sessions. And I would like to continue that trend with you, if I may, Rosie?"

Rosie smiled from one side of her mouth "Yeah. Sure, doc. Whatever you say." She reached across the table and grabbed the file. "May I?" she asked, her eyebrows raised.

"Of course," Mary responded. "It's your information, after all."

Rosie thumbed through the report of the incident and stopped at the page detailing her debriefing. She shook her head and took a deep breath. "Honestly, doc, there's nothing more I can tell you than I have written here. And that's why it is imperative for me to get back to work, so I can begin to fill in these blanks." She closed the file and tossed it back onto the table.

Mary regarded the file for a moment and then made a note on her pad.

Rosie frowned a little at seeing Mary take note of how she discarded the file, but she decided not to say anything. The last thing she needed was to upset the shrink and blow her chance of getting stamped as being fit for service. She was level-headed and not prone to temperamental outbursts, no matter how taxing a suspect or even a colleague could be, so she let it go, as she had many things for the good of getting the upper hand.

Mary finished writing and gently placed the pen back on the pad, then steepled her fingers under her chin again. "You know, combating trauma and returning one's mind to a full and active state can take time, Rosie, and it isn't something that should be rushed, even when the cause is noble. You need to come to terms with the pain and grief that you are clearly dealing with, and even more important is to forgive and absolve yourself of any blame. That way, the true healing can begin, and I believe if you do that it is highly likely your memories will come back to you."

Rosie offered a pained smile. "Look, doc. I appreciate what you are trying to do, honest, I get it and I applaud you. I know it's your job to make sure I'm not mentally damaged by all of this and that I am fit and well to be trusted with returning to the streets with a firearm. I get it." Rosie leaned forward, her elbows on her knees. "But I am a detective who wants nothing more than to get these memories back as soon as possible, so that I can catch this guy. I don't want him to ever hurt anyone again, and believe me, doc, he has hurt many, many people."

Mary took in a deep breath and held it for a few seconds before exhaling through her nose. "I understand that, Rosie, but you need time – time to grieve, in order to heal—"

"I *have* grieved," Rosie blurted, her voice stern and a little too sharp for her own liking. She calmed herself with a small smile. "I have grieved, and I have cried. I went to each of their funerals and grieved again, as God knows that process had been drawn out with the autopsies. I went to their funerals and stood and watched as their loved ones questioned me with their eyes: why was I spared? Why wasn't I in the ground like the others? So right now, as of this moment, all I want to do is get back to work and get my cogs turning I know if I do that, I will get my memory back and I can be of use to my team once again and get the desired answers that *everyone* is looking for. I have to be of use again." She looked up at Mary. "So please… Mary, stamp me fit for duty. Please."

Mary reached down for her pen and scribbled some notes onto her pad. She looked back up with a smile. "So. Tell me. How has your sex life been lately?"

Rosie sat back in her chair sharply, her eyebrows raised.

5

Monday 5th November 2012, Noon.

Sergeant John Walker leant over the precinct front desk and clasped his hands together. "Well, well," he said, smiling and nodding. "Miss Hendricks, if I live and breathe."

"Mr. Walker," she answered with a dutiful nod and a smile.

Returning to a standing position, he waved her through. He held out a hand but Rosie batted it away.

"Give over, Johnny boy. Come on, bring it. Bring… it… in." She held out her arms and hugged him.

John laughed huskily. "It's good to see you, kiddo. How ya feelin'?"

"Ahh, y'know. I'm okay. What about you? Y'alright, big guy?"

He planted his hands on her shoulders. "Better now you're back. Place has been boring without your cheeky ass around."

"Oh, you do have a way with the ladies, Sergeant Walker," she said with a chuckle as she walked away.

"That's what they say, that's what they say," he said with a laugh then returned his attention to his paperwork.

Rosie was still smiling as she walked into the Homicide Office. The cubicle workspaces were deserted, with various screensavers playing out on the computer screens, and on a couple of desks fans whirring back and forth. She frowned and sighed, soaking up the atmosphere of an office in which she spent most of her work-addled, single life. A voice from her left made her head whip around to see the smiling face of Detective Pete Stillman, most likely returning from the kitchen area with a cup of coffee, as he drank nothing else. He gorged on it, in fact – a real aficionado for the stuff. Rosie smiled and waved to him as he approached, planted his mug on a desk, and held his hand out.

"Hendricks. Good to have you back, buddy."

She smacked his hand away with a playful tap. "The hell is it with you guys? Walker just did the damn same." She raised her arms and beckoned him in by wiggling her fingers. "Jesus, forget that shit – bring it in, Stillman."

Pete smiled and switched his offered handshake for a hug; one that carried immense friendship within it.

Sure, Pete and a couple of the other guys had been to visit Rosie while she had been convalescing prior to being cleared for work, but that had been at her apartment, her home, and they had been awkward events. None of them had wished to get into the ins and outs of her current state, or how she had been doing; cops tended to bury their feelings toward each other in the real world. But as Rosie stood hugging her dear friend, any embarrassment to express emotion was gone. The precinct was their sacred ground, their church, and a place where each person would feel the others' pain. It was where their grief for lost comrades, for Larry, could be expressed and where the true healing would begin.

Rosie peeled herself away from Pete and gave him a comforting rub of his shoulder. She looked around. "Where the hell is everybody?"

He raised his eyebrows and followed her gaze around the room. "Ah well, y'know how it is – bad guys to catch 'n all that. Seems to be an influx of the fuckers recently. Keeps us all in work, though, I guess."

She laughed. "Where's Mart?"

He looked back at her. "Probably stuffing his fat face at the vending machine."

Just as Pete finished his playful insult of his partner, Martin Dowd himself walked into the office.

"I heard that, you pencil-thin prick. And for your information, I went to the bathroom." He paused for a second, then grinned. "And then the vending machine."

All three of them laughed, and then Rosie shared an embrace with Martin just as she had with Pete a moment earlier – albeit this time with more vigor from the portly detective.

He pulled away from her and offered a puckered smile. "How ya been, Rosie? Ya feeling better?"

She smiled and reached out to touch his left shoulder. "Yeah. Much better, Mart. Thanks, bud." She tucked her hands into the back pockets of her jeans and motioned over her shoulder with a nod. "Well, I guess I'd best jump straight into it and get back to work."

At that, Pete and Martin offered their agreements and hastily congratulated her again on her return to work, then peeled away to their shared desk.

Captain Banks' commanding voice sounded from his office. "Detective Hendricks, a word please."

"Sir," she acknowledged and made her way to him, making a courteous knock on the doorframe before entering with a smile.

He motioned for her to close the door and then gestured toward a chair.

Before he spoke, Rosie took a few seconds to stare around the room. It was something she always did. It didn't matter that she had been in the office a hundred times, she always stared at the various pictures and commendations that adorned the walls; admiring them. Captain Banks was a person that was easy to admire: a tall, well-built, and gray-haired commanding figure of a man, who knew his job and his people inside out. Everyone respected him, both under his command and higher up, and the praise and adulation for him was well-deserved. Rosie had learned so much from him in the last few years, with him guiding her through the investigations and scenarios where his assistance had been needed the most. Of course, it had been Rosie's acute ability to quickly assimilate and retain information that had made his job much easier, but still, his presence, his guidance and teachings – though often cryptic – had been a great boon to her skill-building within the department. This had undoubtedly contributed to her swiftness in advancement to the rank of detective sergeant.

His chair creaked as he leaned back, bringing her attention back to him. "You look well, Rosie. Much better than when I last saw you."

"Yeah. Yeah. I feel much better, thank you, sir. Been hitting the gym, getting the old reps and times where needed. So, yeah, feeling fightin' fit and raring to go. Dying to get the investigation back underway if I'm being honest."

He nodded, his mouth downturned. "So, what's your first plan of attack? Where you gonna start?"

Her eyes widened. She took a deep breath and leaned forward in her chair. "Well, I wanna review all the audio and video from the night, and start trying to put those pieces together, to help nudge my memory back into place. Then I think I'll hit up the house and retrace my steps."

Captain Banks nodded, the chair creaking in time with his movements. "Solid plan. I'd get on it while you can and get plenty of traction."

She frowned, taken aback a little. "What do you mean, sir, while I can?"

Banks sat forward with a sigh, his elbows on the desk and his hands clasped together. "The case has been flagged nationally, Rosie. The feds are coming in. They're taking it."

She sat up straight. "Oh, you gotta be shittin' me, Captain. Please. Don't let them take it from me. I need this, sir. I need to catch this guy. Me."

He pursed his lips and shook his head. "I'm sorry, Rosie, but it's done. It's out of my hands. Special Agent Denver has been assigned and he'll be arriving Wednesday. He'll be taking the lead on the investigation."

She slumped back in her chair with an aggrieved grunt. "So I'm off it entirely?"

He offered her a sympathetic look. "Uncertain. Denver gets full jurisdiction. And the right to second any member of the team."

Her eyes widened again, and she sat forward.

"It's possible he may want to use you," Banks continued, "but you know the Feds – they tend to want to work under their own steam. I'm sorry, Rosie; it's nothing personal. It's just how it is. But I would use the time you have to become… invaluable." He cocked his head to one side ever so slightly.

She nodded twice, then gave a deep sigh. "What set off the alarm?"

"Well, obviously the amount of media attention the failed grab caught put it on many radars – and once they started checking into it, it became clear that other cases matched the exact same M.O. as your guy."

"Really? How many?"

"A lot!" It was his turn to widen his eyes.

She contemplated him, waiting.

He raised his eyebrows. "Well… you're lucky our national crime databases aren't synced like they should be, or it would have come up sooner, to be honest." He sighed. "Look. You've got a little over twenty-four hours to get your shit together and see what you can learn. Be a team-player, Rosie, and maybe Denver will cut you in."

She nodded several times, then stood up.

"Grab what you need from Evidence, and I believe Forensics are now done with the audio and video, so get them to send over the files."

She pursed her lips and nodded again, then turned to leave.

"And Hendricks?"

She turned to face him.

"Good luck. Let's get a result… for our guys, right?"

She smiled, nodded, then walked back into the main office.

Pete looked up from his desk and furrowed his brow. "Everything okay?"

Rosie nodded and made her way over to her desk, her eyes fixed on the floor. "Yeah, yeah…" She grunted in dissatisfaction and stopped. "Well, no, actually," she said, turning to look at him. "The fucking Feds are taking the case, Pete. I'm losing it to 'em."

Pete sighed and shook his head. "Goddammit. Yeah, I kinda heard something was in the works. Tough break, kiddo. How long ya got?"

She screwed up her mouth and looked up, a little distant. "Twenty-four hours to get my shit together and then probably another twelve to get that shit into a report, give or take; if the fed keeps me around, that is. He's on his way up here Wednesday." She looked at Pete again. "For fuck's sake," she said, spitting out the words with venom, then looking down and jabbing her hands onto her hips. She stared at the ground for a few seconds, contemplative, her eyes darting back and forth as though searching for something out of reach. She closed her eyes, annoyed at the thought of having the case taken from her, at losing the chance to catch the guy, for Larry's sake, for her sake.

Pete's soft, understanding voice brought her out of her musings. "Anything you need, buddy? Anything from me or Mart?"

She looked up to see the genuine concern on his face and, in that moment, she saw that Pete Stillman knew exactly how she felt, that he understood her need to finish what she had started. She shook her head and offered him an uneven smile. "Nah, thanks anyway. Need to grab some files from Forensics and go over everything a few times before he tramples through it all."

Pete nodded and smiled briefly. He raised his eyebrows and smacked his lips. "Well, if you change your mind, just give us a shout. We ain't up to much today, to be fair."

"Thanks," she said as she started to walk away. She stopped and turned back. "I really appreciate that, Pete."

He nodded courteously.

She made to walk away again, then stopped. "Oh, actually, there is one thing. Do you know anyone who can fix fridges? Mine's on the fritz. The damn door keeps opening and I can't afford another one right now."

Pete frowned and looked to one side for a second. "Hmm, you could try Phil in Motor Pool. You know, the one who—"

"—who seems to have a thing for me?" she said with a dry laugh.

"No *seems* about it, Hendricks... he *has* a thing for you." Pete laughed. "I dunno if he could for sure, but he's a pretty handy guy. He fixed the aircon in the building last summer, if you remember?"

She did. It had been hot as hell, and the certified air-conditioning maintenance company for the precinct had been inundated with repair requests and had a huge backlog. Everyone had been incredibly grateful to 'Phil in Motor Pool' for pulling off that little miracle

"Although," Pete continued with a frown, "I got a feeling he might be on vacation for another week still. Sorry. But you should check with Traffic all the same."

"Shit," she said. "Okay. Thanks anyway, buddy."

He nodded and turned back to his work as Rosie walked to her desk. It was reflective of her personality: incredibly neat and highly organized. Its surface was clear, with any pertinent casefiles seated in wallets within the big bottom drawer and her in-tray consisting of a modest, neatly-stacked pile of paperwork. Not being one for knick-knacks, there were no cute items, decorations, or pictures on the desk, just a pen holder containing colored pens and highlighters, along with a stapler and a triangular desk calendar to the side. Her desktop computer monitor and a phone were situated to the right side of the desk.

Rosie plonked herself into the swivel chair and drew herself up to the desk, then picked up the phone and punched three numbers.

After a few rings, a female voice answered, "Forensics, Pearl speaking."

"Hey Pearl, Hendricks here—"

Before Rosie could continue, Pearl interrupted. "Oh hi, Rosie. How are you, honey? Good to have you back and up on your feet. Hope you're feeling much better."

Rosie liked Pearl. She was a jolly woman, who always had a smile and laugh for anyone who called in to see her or phoned, especially if it was one of the girls. Even though Rosie had no love of gossip, she was always entertained by Pearl's attitude toward it, and found herself tuning in for way longer than she would if it were anyone else. But today, she didn't feel much like 'shootin' the shit' with her, and so she decided to move the conversation on as quickly as she could.

"I'm fine, Pearl, honest. Just glad to get back to work and at it – y'know, for Larry's sake." Rosie imagined Pearl sitting up: she gave a small "Oh" in response.

"I hear ya," Pearl said. "Whaddaya need?"

Rosie had felt a little guilty for cutting her short, but it was clear Pearl understood. "Ummm, I need the forensics report, together with the audio and video for 11089. Any chance you could email all the files to me ASAP?"

"Course, sweetie," came Pearl's prompt, formal reply. "I'll have them sent over within the hour."

"Thanks Pearl, you're a star, hon."

"Anytime, sugar," Pearl replied before hanging up.

Rosie replaced the receiver, grabbed a pen from the holder, and began to chew on the end while leaning back in her chair and swiveling.

6

Monday 5th November 2012, 10.00pm.

Rosie kicked the apartment door open with a tad too much force and it smashed into the wall. "Goddammit," she said, fumbling with the keys in one hand and a small brown bag filled with milk and bread held in the other arm. She entered and fiddled at the bottom of the door with her foot, then kicked it shut, with the same force as she had opened it. She rolled her eyes at the loud bang it made. She then cast her eye on the area of damage the handle had made; there was no doorstop to prevent it hitting the wall and it had indented an imprint into it. She grunted in anger, then sighed and walked over to her desk situated next to the small, two-person dining table in her living space. She plonked the brown bag onto it, took her handbag from her shoulder and draped it over her desk chair, then picked up the small bag of groceries and sniffed the air as a foul, pungent odor stung her nostrils. The smell drew her attention to the kitchen area. Frowning, she approached it and saw the fridge door open, the strips of duct tape now dangling. In front of the fridge and strewn over the floor were its contents, the food already rotten and flies buzzing around. The smell intensified, and she retched. Suddenly, she dropped the bag containing the milk and bread as a whispered – yet loud – voice from behind made her wheel around and draw her gun.

"I see you!" it said, sly and malevolent, drawing out the words.

She trained her Glock 22 handgun left and right, checking each corner of the room as she edged toward her front door, then reached out with her left hand to confirm that it was locked. She proceeded to check each room in the apartment, taking great care to clear her corners and around the doors as though this were a bust in someone else's apartment. At last, and satisfied that she was alone, she holstered the firearm, cursing to herself for allowing her mind to trick her into thinking she had heard someone speak. There must have been some other logical explanation. Making her way back to her kitchen, she stopped dead. Where the rotten and decaying food had sat, the area was clean, the fridge door closed, the pieces of tape intact and holding the door shut. She peered over the kitchen counter that separated the two rooms and checked the floor. The bag of milk and bread was no longer on the ground where she had dropped it; instead, as her gaze shifted to the table beside her desk with the laptop on it, she saw that the bag was back where she had placed it – except it was neatly flattened and the produce was beside it. She ran an unsteady finger across her top lip and looked around, her eyes watering and extreme doubt and confusion creeping in. She cast her mind back to her conversations with Dr. Williams during their back-to-work session. Williams had told her that what she had experienced during the incident was going to take time, and that her mind might deal with it in very strange ways, often manifesting as severe psychological issues much later.

She closed her eyes and took deep breaths, then moved toward the table and picked up the carton of milk. She examined it, then did the same with the bread. Sighing, she made her way tentatively to the fridge, peeled away the tape and opened the door, placing the milk inside. She closed and resealed the door with the strips of tape, put the bread on the work surface, then turned around, and leaned against it, pondering.

Was this what Williams meant? That her grief and trauma had manifested in this way? She had been used to seeing all kinds of crazy things in the past, given the shit that people pulled in her line of work, but this had felt different; weird, even. Her finger once again ran back and forth over her top lip, as she often had when she had been nervous or stressed as a child. She hadn't done this in years and as soon as she spotted she was doing it, she stopped, forcefully dragging her hand away.

She looked back toward the fridge and folded her arms. "Goddammit, Rosie," she said in a huff with herself. "You're losing your fucking mind. Now stop it; stupid bitch."

As hard as Rosie would be on suspects and, in some instances, her own staff, such behavior paled into insignificance compared to how hard she was on herself when she felt she was letting herself down, not commanding a situation well, or not being thorough enough with her own reasoning. She scolded herself internally, annoyed at her bewilderment and for allowing herself to feel frightened, even for a moment. She hated uncertainty and not knowing when it came to investigations or anything else she was involved with, and she had, over the years, come to trust her own instincts implicitly, so the sensation she had felt and was *still* feeling – brooding doubt, hints of losing her mind and the crushing loneliness due to Larry's absence – scared her.

She closed her eyes and shook her head, then began rummaging through her cupboards to find something to make for supper.

****

The laptop screen illuminated her face as she stared at it, having lowered the lights in the apartment to a subtler hue. She had set about compiling the start of her report as best as she could, attempting to describe how things had gone down and consolidate the confusing information from the sniper nests, about how they could see the perp through thermals. But in the end had concluded she was no more the wiser than she ever had been, and the only way she could begin to piece it all together would be to sift through the footage and audio evidence when Forensics eventually got their shit together and sent her the files. She grumbled at that thought. Why was it taking them so long? Pearl had said she would send it within the hour. Rosie needed the info and it was painful waiting. But she knew that it was just another thing Forensics had to do among thousands of other things, and she would just have to wait her turn – especially since they operated for more than just her precinct. They had a dozen others under their wing, all with priority cases of their own.

With a deep groan she leaned back and stretched, only then realizing she still had her empty supper bowl in her lap; she grabbed it as the spoon threatened to topple out and onto the floor, then placed it and the bowl on the dining table. She then leaned back in her chair and allowed herself the stretch she so desperately needed, working out the kinks and knots of the day's stress. She closed the lid of her laptop, then stood, grabbed the bowl and marched it to the sink where she dropped it inside; the spoon rattling around as she did. Turning on the hot water faucet, she ran some water into the bowl and left it to soak; she was too tired and irritated to clean up even one small item. She then made her way to the bathroom. At the start of the corridor, she turned and glanced at the fridge. It sat there as it always had. Nothing moving, no open door, no food popping out. She wondered if she had imagined the strange event when she had first returned to her apartment; whether the tape slapped across the door and side was a pointless item, and there had been nothing wrong with the fridge at all. Perhaps everything she thought had been wrong was within her own mind and nothing more.

She grunted and shook her head, then traipsed to the bathroom, stopping in its doorway to consider whether she would have a shower or a bath. She pursed her lips, pondering.

Fuck it! she told herself, *a bath is too much hassle. I'll have a quick shower and get to bed. Don't wanna be tired before Special Agent Scott fucking Denver arrives with his super-dooper bureau skills. Asshole.* Even within her mind, the final word had venom, reflecting her belief that the whole F.B.I. thing existed only to screw her over – at least, it felt that way. She shook her head, then reached into the shower and turned it on. Steam filled the room fast, and she had to wipe the mirror squeakily with the back of her hand to see herself. She screwed up her face.

"Pure and utter man-bait, Hendricks," she said, then added the word 'not' as the steam once more obscured her reflection from existence. She shook her head again stripped naked and got into the shower, wincing slightly at the temperature of the water, though it only took a few seconds for her body to adjust.

It felt like she had been in the shower for hours when she finally decided to get out, although in truth it had only been about 15 mins. Rather than cleaning herself, most of that time had been spent thinking about Larry. Thinking, and crying. She had tried to block the grief from her mind by diving into her work or postulating about the case; anything to get the image of Larry's final moments – the look of sheer terror on his face as he had been sucked through the door – out of her mind. Certain moments from the disastrous event had started to return to her, and that had been one of the strongest images, although it was one she wanted least, and it took great effort to keep forcing it from her psyche. She wondered if she ever might succeed in doing so, ever. With a slam of her hand against the shower wall, she turned off the water, and reached out to fumble for the towel hanging outside. She wrapped it around herself, drew the curtain back and stepped out, then leaned over the bath to wring her hair as dry as possible. Finally, she grabbed a smaller towel and wrapped it around her head, then wiped the mirror, her hand squeaking on its surface again. She gazed at the sullen face that stared back at her, noting its forlorn expression. She looked a hundred years old. The past weeks had indeed taken their toll, but even so, her grief had made her determined – or perhaps it was just what she deserved – to look and feel like shit. She looked into the sink bowl and allowed herself another little cry.

Having regained her composure with a resolute and forceful grunt, she opened the mirrored cabinet door, reached for her toothbrush and toothpaste, then closed the door and stared at her misty self again. The steam once more threatened to dominate the surface and so she wiped at it again with the back of her hand that held the brush.

As she did, the brush handle clipped the side of the cabinet and it tumbled out of her hand and onto the floor. Annoyed, Rosie bent down to pick it up.

As Rosie stood, she startled as she thought she caught a glimpse of a large human form in the mirror and stood behind her. She turned around quickly. Nobody was there but she then felt cold air suddenly snake its way across her shoulders and down her back. She whirled around to face the mirror again and then her attention snapped to the window to her left, assuming she had left it open. It was shut. Frowning, she turned back to the mirror slowly, then squirted toothpaste onto her brush and cleaned her teeth. She couldn't help but check behind herself a couple of times as she continued to ponder what she thought she saw. When she was finished, she reached into the cabinet again for night moisturizer and applied it to her face.

Ablution routine completed, she headed to the kitchen, filled a glass with water, took a sip, then made her way to the living room and began turning off the lights. Trudging down the hall to her bedroom, she flicked off the last switch to plunge the remaining section into darkness.

At the end of the corridor and watching Rosie close the door to her bedroom, the silhouetted form of a man dominated the space, his shoulders heaving up and down.

****

Rosie opened her eyes, pulled out of her slumber suddenly rather than her usual steady waking. She felt uneasy, sensing a presence, but a quick glance around her room revealed nothing other than irregular shadows cast by the meagre moonlight. The room felt cold – *very* cold – and she wondered if she might have left a window open, a notion that seemed confirmed as she glanced at the white net curtains covering the large window, fluttering gently as though a light breeze disturbed them. But the window wasn't open; she knew it absolutely, and dismissed the thought – she wouldn't open it at this time of year, hating the cold as she did. Even so, the room felt icy cold against her cheeks and as she breathed out, her breath became a billowing mist that took much longer than normal to dissipate. She wanted to move, to sit upright, but she couldn't; her body was locked in place with irrational fear. Then her breathing became shallow and a lump formed in the center of her chest, a tense knot that felt as though it were burrowing deep, trying to push into her lungs and prevent her from breathing altogether. Goosebumps raised all over her body as yet another chill snaked its way over her. She had never felt irrational fear as profound as this in adult life, or felt so helpless as she did now. Her police training and the composure borne from it was utterly useless. Her eyes watered. Was she going to cry? Was this insane fear, of which she had no understanding, becoming so crippling that it would debilitate her completely?

She tried to take a deep breath, to force herself into a reality other than the one that had her gripped, but it proved to be of no help. At that moment she considered whether this was all a dream, wondering whether she was experiencing sleep paralysis, a phenomenon she had once read about. But she knew that her thoughts were too real and too precise to reflect such a state. She understood that she was awake and that something terrible was preventing her from functioning normally.

As Rosie shifted her attention away from her net curtains, her gaze drifted past a chair in the corner of her room, where she would normally throw her clothes. She gasped and her attention snapped back to it. Someone was sitting on it. It appeared to be a teenage child – a girl, from what Rosie could make out, although she couldn't be certain, as that corner of the room was much darker than elsewhere. In fact, she came to the conclusion that the corner appeared much darker than she had ever remembered it being. Then the thought occurred to her that she was probably staring at her clothing, positioned in such a way that it made it look like a person. She narrowed her eyes to confirm that she was being nothing more than a stupid woman letting her mind run away from her.

Then the figure opened its neon-white eyes.

Rosie snapped her eyes shut tight, gave a terrified yelp, and began to pant. Her mind raced at what she had just witnessed: the creepiness of what could only be a ghost child in her room. What the hell was happening to her?

Her eyes snapped open and widened. She held her breath as the latch to her wardrobe door to her right chinked, then the door creaked open – but her attention was still on the chair, which was now empty once again.

She gasped. Notwithstanding the fact that the latch had lifted, her fear had spiked due to the movement of the door, which had to be deliberate, such was the stiffness of the old, antiquated piece of furniture that once belonged to her grandmother. It simply could not open of its own accord. Something had to pull it; or worse… push. She forced her eyes shut, tears beading. Gritting her teeth, and growing increasingly angrier at her inability to act, she breathed out hard and reopened her eyes, then turned to look. Sure enough, the wardrobe door was ajar. She yelped a little as a ghostly male voice whispered from the crack.

"He's coming for you. He wants you. Soon, Rosie, soon."

The wardrobe door creaked open further, the sound both terrifying and irritating. Rosie's body went rigid, and her fingers twitched against her thighs, her arms locked straight by her sides. She could do nothing but stare into the growing darkness as the door continued to open gradually, prolonging her terror and the uncertainty of what was causing it to move. A million thoughts raced through her mind, some transporting her back to her childhood and the fear of monsters lurking in her closet. Her mind continued to conjure all the things that might be inside and trying to creep out, but then locked onto the strongest thought of all: an intruder that had been here all along and was now messing with her. The fridge, the food… everything. An assailant that had been in her apartment for days, maybe even weeks, skulking out of sight and taking his time to plot all the horrific things he was going to do. Her terror piqued as the door creaked to a halt, now wide open and presenting a large rectangle of black from which she expected to see a demented face emerge at any moment. Her eyes watered even more.

Somewhere within her, a spark of courage ignited, and a hint of composure returned. She didn't know why it was happening at that moment – her trepidation at what might be staring at her from the

40

blackness of the wardrobe still gnawed inside her, and her terror still lingered – but whatever it was, she wasn't going to let the feeling pass without acting on it. She forced her gaze away from the darkness and to her bedside table. She always housed her gun in its top drawer while she slept. If she could just pull herself together enough to move her arms, she would reach for it and feel safe, knowing she could defend herself from anything. But as quickly as her bravery arrived, her vulnerability returned once more. Shuffling from within the wardrobe brought new terror, and once more she fought back tears. The sound continued, as though something inside was creeping toward her, although the wardrobe was not as deep as the prolonged and echoing noise suggested. She began to hyperventilate as her fear continued to lock her in place, awaiting whatever was coming.

Then she heard a young girl crying and whimpering, followed by the child's voice saying one word: "No."

Suddenly, the pressure lifted from her chest, as though a hand that had been pushing her down into the bed had been removed. She sat bolt upright and inhaled deep, like breaking the surface of water moments before running out of oxygen. Her hands clasped to her chest as she stared wide-eyed at the white lace curtains that continued to dance in some ethereal wind. Then she whipped her head to the right, to the darkness of the wardrobe. But the door was shut; there were no sounds and no voice.

Rosie began to sob, drawing her knees up to her chest and burying her head in the bed covers.

Clung to the wall like Christ on the cross and behind a sobbing Rosie, a man dressed all in black, with a long black overcoat, his jet black and greasy straggled hair almost covering his chalky white face watched her through piercing yellow, cat-like eyes. And he smiled. Wide. Baring horrific sharp, crooked, and broken teeth set behind blood-red lips. He looked down at her, the movement slow and deliberate, his smile widening, creepy and unnatural, then spun slowly to the left and into an inverted cross position above her.

Rosie felt a chill race down her spine. A malevolent cold that suggested something very wrong was happening around her. She gasped and scrambled forward in the bed, then turned to look at the wall. But there was nothing there, save for handprints partway up, which then faded.

7

Wednesday 7th November 2012, 10.00am.

Seated at her desk in the detective's office at the precinct, Rosie rubbed her eyes with her thumb and forefinger. She felt like shit and wondered if that had translated to her appearance.

The past couple of days had taken their toll. She had worked tirelessly to gather as much information as possible before the Fed showed up. Because of his imminent arrival, she had spent more time than usual that morning grooming herself in front of the mirror, applying a greater than usual amount of make-up in an attempt to conceal the increasingly dark rings under her eyes. But eventually, she had said "Fuck it" and accepted this was as good as she would get, and headed to work.

The drive had been torturous, not least the delays caused by a swell of traffic due to a burst water main, but also because her brain would not let the events of the previous night go. It was what she did: overanalyze every detail to try to draw sense from any experience or event. The fear she had felt during the night perplexed her. Sure, she was a cop, but she was also human, and last night had been different. In all her years since childhood and its plague of irrational fears, she had never experienced ones so tangible that she could almost taste them. The terror had been palpable – arresting, even – and she had succumbed to it entirely.

She mulled over the strange events that had been happening all week. The fridge, the weird visions, the feeling of someone being around her although just out of reach and unseen, skulking in the shadows at the periphery of her vision. So many times, she had felt a presence only for her to see nothing upon turning. However, in those instances she hadn't experienced fear, more curiosity, her training overwhelming her irrationality, but last night's events had been quite different. The sense of real and terrible danger had been so overpowering it had paralyzed her, something a cop absolutely did not want to feel in a high-pressure situation. It had left her feeling powerless, useless, and she needed to know why. It was also the reason, during the drive, she had contemplated calling Dr. Williams and booking another session, but then dismissed it as foolish weakness, such was her pride.

She looked up and yawned as Pete ambled over and placed a large mug of coffee on her desk.

"Jesus, Hendricks, did you even sleep last night? You look like shit."

"Thanks, Pete," she said, her shoulders slumping. She gave him a disdainful look. "That's exactly the kind of pep talk to get a girl on her feet in a morning. Yay!" She waved her hands in the air sarcastically.

Pete chuckled and moved to his desk a few feet away from hers. Sitting, he swiveled in his chair so that he faced her. She huffed a laugh as she watched him blow into his mug and then take a sip. She contemplated him for a few seconds before softening her tone to say, "I tried, Pete, I really tried, but I kept on having the weirdest dreams and sensations. At least, I *hope* they were dreams."

His head jerked up. He furrowed his brow and pressed his lips tight together. "The fuck does that mean, you hope they were dreams?"

She stared, rolling her tongue and then biting her bottom lip. She took a breath. "Okay. Don't look at me like I'm going crazy when I tell you this, but I saw stuff last night, and I heard Larry's voice, calling my name and saying stuff – but his voice was all weird and shit." She paused and looked away briefly before continuing. "It all started out mild at first, a word here and there, but then, at one point—" she looked down, "—well, at one point, honestly, I thought I was flat-out losing my shit."

"You are!" he said and snorted a laugh.

"Oh, ha ha, thanks, pal. But seriously, Pete, it's been so weird over the last few weeks and stuff keeps moving around on its own in my apartment."

He stared at her for a moment, mouth open, eyes wide. Then he burst into laughter.

"Oh, fuck you, Stillman! I knew you wouldn't believe me." She turned away, more disappointed than annoyed. Pete was a good friend and he usually had her back when it came to her voicing her opinions. To have him dismiss her so easily and with such a mocking reaction saddened her, and she didn't want him to see disappointment on her face – not least because she had her own doubts about what had happened and the last thing she needed was him noticing. She sighed and let her head flop forward, then looked up as Pete approached her desk and sat down on the edge of it. He flashed an apologetic smile at her, which made her feel instantly better.

"Look, buddy. I'm sorry, that was shitty of me and I apologize for laughing. I also don't think you're crazy. The bottom line is you've been through one hell of an ordeal and you have to be suffering from all sorts of shit because of it. Grief, rage, and probably depression. All these things hitting you in spades because of what happened to our guys and the fact you can't stop blaming yourself."

She began to protest, but he laid a gentle hand on her shoulder.

"Our guys, Rosie… yeah. The level of responsibility you're feeling is manifesting itself as tricks of the mind. Honestly, it's only natural – and I should know, as I've been through something similar."

She looked at him, eyes wide, and was about to say something when he cut her short.

"Hey, look. Just because I don't spill every little detail of my life doesn't mean shit hasn't happened to me before."

She realized she may have been about to say something dumb, so clamped her mouth shut.

Pete looked at his hands as he fiddled with them. "I lost a partner before Martin, you know."

She hadn't known that, and she knew that her expression conveyed as much.

"Yeah," he said, nodding. "Shook me to the core. Took me months to even begin to come to terms with it, let alone get over it. That shit took me years." He half-smiled. "Blamed myself, of course. A lot. Couple weeks after the incident I started seeing him everywhere. And I mean *everywhere*. In the car, at the store, at the bar. Everywhere. I'd hurry over to him, smiling, ecstatic, thinking I was gonna see him again, even though the rational part of my mind kept telling me it was impossible. And, sure enough, upon reaching him it turned out to be someone else. Looking at me totally confused, because I'd rambled at them for a few seconds as though I was talking to him again." He glanced at her and twitched a smile. "Eventually, when I just let go and

44

got on with my life, I stopped seeing him. Still think about him often, though. Danny Palazzo. Great guy, awesome bro, and a superb cop." He stared ahead for a few moments, locked in reminiscence.

Rosie silently mouthed a few words before finding her voice. "Pete. I'm... I'm so sorry. I didn't know. You've never mentioned it. I've never heard you say anything quite like that before now." She knew she was blustering, the situation having made her uncomfortable, as though it should be something she should have known all along and she was letting him down. She stared at the ground.

"Hey, seriously, Rosie, it's fine. I'm all done with that side of the process now. But my point is, you gotta see this for what it is. Grief. Nothing more, nothing less. Okay?"

She smiled a little. "Yeah." She nodded a few times. "Yeah, I hear ya." She contemplated Pete's words as he started to get up, then she stopped him. "Hey, Pete. Thanks, man."

He smiled and nodded, then retreated to his desk to resume sipping his coffee, stabbing a key on his computer to bring it to life.

A soft ping from Rosie's own computer indicated she had mail. She swung her chair, then rattled the mouse, firing the monitor into life.

"About goddamn time," she said, double-clicking the email and hovering her mouse over each of the four folders in turn: *HIGH-GROUND#1, HIGH-GROUND#2, S.W.A.T., COMMAND VEHICLE.*

She double clicked *HIGH-GROUND#1*, then scrambled around her desk for her headphones; then double-clicked on *VIDEO + AUDIO.* She watched as the screen displayed the thermal image captured by Gerry, then she narrowed her eyes as the picture focused on a section of the outside wall of the house before the conversation between her and Gerry began:

"Wait! What the fuck?"

"What? What is it, Taylor?"

Lieutenant Phillips' voice cut in. *"Entry teams hold."*

A brief silence played out and Rosie remembered that was the point Lieutenant Phillips had tried to scold her for talking to the teams instead of him. Then her voice cut in again.

"Talk to me, Taylor – what's going on?"

"I can see the guy, Hendricks."

"What?"

"This shouldn't be possible, but I can see the guy, I can see his thermal image in my scope through the fucking wall."

Hearing the moment play out was jarring, and it set cogs whirring in her mind. She had begun to remember snippets of the night, but hearing her exchange with Gerry pushed memories right to the forefront. She was starting to remember. She nodded a couple of times, then moved the slider at the bottom of the video playback along a few frames. She would come back to the whole recording again later, to make detailed notes, but for now she needed to check through it quickly. She let it go and resumed playback as Gerry and Donny began to converse:

"Donny, I am telling you I can see the fucker, sat down in a chair in his fucking living room."

"You're freaking me out, Ger. IR don't see through walls or windows."

"Don't you think I fucking know that Donny. S'why I'm freaking out myself, but I'm telling you I can see him…"

It appeared that Gerry cut his sentence short. There was a short silence before Donny's voice kicked back in.

"Ger. Ger, you there. Talk to me, man!"

Another short silence before Gerry's voice resumed.

"Whoa, wait, wait – I've got two targets now. What the fuck! I have two tangos. I repeat, another tango was sat on top of the fucker and has got up and is moving toward the east wall."

Rosie's voice came through.

"What do you mean, Gerry? We got nothing here. Confirm, over?"

Next it was Sergeant Barnes' voice.

"What's happening Command? You callin' it or what, over?"

The conversation between Gerry and Donny resumed.

"High Ground Two, you seeing this, over?"

"Nothing, I got nothing, High Ground One. What are you seei—"

Rosie winced as Donny's scream pierced her ears. She pressed the pause button and closed her eyes, rubbing her forehead and taking a deep breath, then exhaling slowly. Her mouth felt dry, though she could feel saliva within it. She swallowed hard a few times and then coughed as she felt a tickle at the back of her throat. She then opened the *HIGH-GROUND#2* folder and scrolled to the same timeline point as when Gerry began to report seeing the perp on thermal imaging, but saw nothing that would explain it, and so went back to Gerry's file and reviewed it intently up to the same point, taking detailed notes. This

46

was how she worked, splitting evidence into chunks, reviewing and taking her time not to miss anything before moving on.

As she reviewed the footage from Gerry's camera at the point he started ID'ing the guy, the screen began to flicker and distort as though a magnet had been drawn across it. Rosie frowned as the image continued to behave erratically. When she reached out to touch it, she lurched and cried out as a hand grabbed her shoulder. Wheeling around, she saw a man standing before her, smartly dressed in a grey suit and with immaculate swept-back dark hair.

"Detective Sergeant Hendricks?" he asked.

She closed her eyes and placed a hand on her chest, then took off her headphones. "Jesus H. fucking Christ. You scared the shit outta me!"

The man smiled at her. It was a pleasant one – charming, even – and all at once she noticed how attractive he was, with brilliant white teeth and a stubble-free face. She ran the numbers on him: mid-thirties, ambitious, career-driven, probably good with the ladies. *The Fed,* she thought.

"Sorry. Didn't mean to startle you." He smiled again. "I called out a couple of times but you had your headphones on. Sorry to have to grab you."

She shook her head and huffed a small laugh. She liked how he talked: gruff, with a cool tone to his voice. A bit like Josh Brolin, and she loved herself a bit of Josh Brolin.

"Ahh, forget about it," she said, standing up. "I was just – oh, well, it doesn't matter." She held out a hand. "Yeah, I'm Detective Sergeant Hendricks. And you must be Special Agent Scott Denver."

He took her hand and shook it. "That I am, detective sergeant. And I am pleased to meet you."

Rosie scoffed. "Ugh, call me Rosie, for God's sake. I'm about to get screwed, so you might as well use my first name."

Scott offered a small, slightly embarrassed smile. "Well, okay then, and you can call me Scott. Also, no-one is screwing anyone. Well, y'know, not unless they want to…"

Rosie laughed and held up a hand. "Okay, okay. You got banter, I'll give you that, Denver."

He smiled again. "Scott. Please." He pursed his lips and nodded.

She nodded. "Scott it is."

Scott glanced around the room and then back at Rosie "Truth is, Rosie, I really need your expertise here, and I am very keen to hear your account of the situation personally. Everything you have learned."

She rippled air out through her lips while glancing upward. "Well, that's not a lot, I can tell you."

"Even so. I believe that Captain Banks has advised our two agencies will be working together on this?"

She nodded. "He has. But not to what level."

He smiled again. "Well, just to put your mind at rest, I want you working alongside me in full. I've read some of the reports you put together prior to the unfortunate arrest attempt and it truly is exceptional police work. So yeah, I need some of that expertise if we are to catch this maniac."

She took a deep breath and gave a smile of relief. "Well… that'll be my pleasure, Scott. My absolute pleasure."

He gave a small nod.

She suddenly realized she had been staring at him too long without speaking, so she continued, "Err, okay. Well, let me get my files and laptop, then we can go grab a coffee." She looked around. "Something better than this place offers, at least." She smiled. "And maybe some lunch as well and get to it. You at a hotel nearby?"

He nodded. "Yeah. Just a couple of blocks down. Pretty convenient."

"Y'all checked in?"

He nodded again. "Checked in, bags dropped, and ready to go, sergeant." He smiled. "I mean Rosie."

She laughed. "Okay, great. Well, let's get after it, then."

8

Wednesday 7th November 2012, 10.30am.

Good looking, and a gentleman, Rosie thought as Scott held open the door to the diner for her. Working with her male counterparts for so many years, she hadn't experienced many chivalrous moments. It wasn't that her colleagues were not gentlemen – far from it – it was more that they had never seen her as anything other than one of them. They had manners, but wouldn't necessarily hold the door for her to go through, rather, they'd go through and then hold it for her to take. There was a difference. Scott's little act of kindness hadn't gone unnoticed, as normal and innocuous it would be to most other people. But cops were not like other people.

She nodded as he pointed to a booth well out of the way of the diner's other occupants, aware that would be best given the sensitive nature of the material they would be discussing. Approaching it, she took off her suit jacket and laid it neatly on the seat, pushing it up and out of the way, then slipped into the booth. Scott did the same on the opposite side, but leaving his jacket on. She offered him a *well-this-is-nice* sort of smile as a middle-aged waitress approached, notepad and pencil raised.

"Hey, Rosie," the waitress said, her smile warm and friendly.

Rosie smiled back at her. She glanced around. "Hey, Shirl. Kinda slow today, huh?"

Shirley wrinkled her nose. "Ah, it's in between that period of breakfast and lunch, y'know. Besides, don't often see you in here at this hour. Kinda how it is at this time, I guess."

Rosie nodded a couple of times, continuing to survey the room as if to validate Shirley's claim.

"Anyway," Shirley said, with another smile, "what'll you and your handsome friend here have?"

Rosie clucked her tongue and gave a wry smile as she looked down at the table. "Not like that, Shirl. It's a work thing."

Shirley giggled. "Oh, I know, sweetie, just passing the time with some fun. All you cops look the same anyways." She smirked.

Rosie turned her attention to Scott. "You want any food?"

He contemplated this for a second, his lips pursed, then shook his head. "Nah, coffee'll be fine. Espresso with an added double shot, please." He smiled at Shirley.

Rosie raised her eyebrows. "Wow. Sleep much?" She chuckled.

He huffed a laugh. "Do any of us?"

Rosie mulled her response, raising her eyebrows as she turned back to Shirley. "Usual for me, Shirl. Thanks."

"Okie dokie," the waitress replied, jotting down the order and then toddling off to the counter to hand the receipt to the barista.

Scott made a show of observing the diner, eyebrows raised, mouth puckered and head nodding. "So, this is the place, eh?" he said, then tutted. "Where West Babylon P.D. hang out?"

"Yep. This is the place. Good coffee. Food's so-so. Usually get pizza at Gino's a few blocks down when we wanna eat out. Take it you have somewhere like this?"

He turned back to her and smiled.

She chuckled and shuffled in her seat, leaning forward a little. "Ah, okay – enough with this small-talk bullshit. Let's get into what we came here to do."

Scott nodded, then reached down to retrieve his briefcase, laying it gently on the table and clicking both latches open at the same time. Rosie followed suit; the only difference being that her files were held in a medium-sized satchel.

Scott placed a series of brown kraft paper folders onto the table and dropped his hands onto them. "Okay. So why don't you bring me up to speed with where you are, and what you've got, and I'll see if I can fill in a few blanks."

"Fair enough," she replied, cocking her head to one side and sorting through her own folders. She then gently closed the one she had opened as Shirley approached with their coffees, and smiled at the waitress. "Ah, cheers honey, that's great."

"You're welcome, sweetie," Shirley replied, "and there's sugar there if you need it." She pointed to a dispenser to one side of the table, beside the wall.

"Ah, I'm good, thanks," Scott said then looked at Rosie, who shook her head.

"Not me. Sweet enough." Rosie turned her attention to Shirley. "Got some stuff to do, honey, so if you could keep the coast clear for us for a while, that'd be great."

Another Shirley-smile. "Course, sweetie. Just holler if you need a refill."

Rosie smiled back and nodded. She waited for Shirley to move far enough away then reopened her case file and took a swig of her coffee, swishing it around her mouth before swallowing. She leafed through a few pages of briefs before clearing her throat.

"Okay, so. Our investigations have three victims on the books, the crimes all occurring within three weeks of one another. At first we believed our guy was working a weekly cycle, but since nobody's been murdered with the same M.O. since our failed grab, I'm discounting that theory and looking for other cycles."

Rosie then reached over and took another swig from her cup, once again taking time to savor the flavor and While she drank, Scott pondered her for a moment; attempting to get a clear read. He would often pride himself on his perception when analyzing people, but for some reason he was struggling to get the measure of her. Normally even a limited interaction would be enough for him to start formulating some sort of picture, but with her it was different. He sensed that doing so would produce immediate incorrect results that he would have to walk back in his mind a short time later. And he didn't want to do that. Didn't want to second guess her backstory, or her nature. He found the predicament quite curious. A part of him made the argument that his difficulty was due to his attraction to her, and he found himself shifting in his seat. Maybe he was tired from the journey, and his lack of sleep over the last week. He fidgeted again, returning his attention to her as she continued.

"Unfortunately, with all that said, it has put me back to square one with this guy's pattern. So, what else do I know?" Rosie looked up at him, then immediately back to her files, the question evidently rhetorical. "Well, what is consistent is the perp's M.O., and the way in which he kills." She opened another folder and pulled out three photographs which she spread out in front of her, upside down so that Scott could view them. "As you can see, each victim was stripped naked and mutilated. Two of the victims were male and one female." She glanced up at him. "In case you're struggling to tell from these shots – Lord knows I'd struggle if I hadn't attended the scene." She looked back at the photos. "And each suffered major trauma to various limbs." She shuffled one of the photos around to look at it, then placed it back. "Yeah – and in all cases their arms were dislocated and wrenched across their backs, and their hands placed together over their buttocks. Our perp then secured them with a railway spike, hammered through the hands and into the body just above the coccyx."

She took a moment to glance up at Scott and gauge his reaction, but he seemed unfazed by the gruesome images and so returned to describing them, though she had a feeling his information would overlap hers. "Next, he dislocated the legs at the hip and bent them backwards, angled outward away from the head – and we both know, that would take some fucking effort." She glanced up at him again. "Then, each foot was nailed to the floor with yet more railway spikes." She took another swig of coffee. "I can tell you with absolute certainty, Agent Denver, I have never seen anything so horrific done to another human being in my entire career. Nobody on my team had, or anyone who attended the scene. Some of the newer guys were sick. Hell, I felt sick."

Scott puckered his lips and nodded. "Okay. That all?"

Rosie shook her head. She pulled out another series of photos depicting the bodies with the spikes removed and the limbs back in their normal positions. "As you can see, the perp carved pentagrams into the back of each victim, and some strange symbols that we are having all sorts of trouble identifying. Obviously, our assessment is that the murders are satanic and ritualistic in nature." She pointed to the symbols in turn. "We've run these past the experts we have access to, and the closest that a couple got to describing them was that they appear Aramaic, and revolve around the summoning of dark forces. That's all they could say without any more context or detail."

Scott nodded. "Yeah, Aramaic can be a pretty tricky language to translate."

Her attention snapped to him, although he didn't notice as he was still studying the photos. She was getting excited: she felt she was about to learn a hell of a lot more than she knew already. Cops are used to seeing horrible shit, but his demeanor was more of acceptance and validation; a strange sort of excitement of his own, although contained. *A true Fed*, she thought.

Scott picked up one of the photos and held it to the light. "And even then, it can depend on the perception of the translator and the positions of the symbols, which can massively skew the meaning."

"You seem very well informed, Agent Denver," Rosie said, raising her eyebrows.

Scott smiled. "Well, in fairness, Rosie, I am a little further down the tracks than you, but only because we have more vics. So, anything else?"

She studied him for a moment, then jerked as though someone had prodded her. "Oh, er, yeah. Here." She took out more photographs and yet again laid them out for him to see. "The shots from the front. As you can see, he slit them from the middle of the neck all the way down to the base of their stomachs. He then removed their hearts." She looked up at Scott. "We never found those at the scene, so we can only assume he collects them as trophies."

Again, Scott pursed his lips and nodded.

Rosie pointed to one of the photographs. "He also removed their eyes. We believe he did that because of, well, windows to the soul and all that. We have nothing more to go on, in that respect. So, there you have it. All pretty harrowing and very grisly. Enough to ensure you never sleep again, no matter what line of work you're in."

Scott took a deep and contemplative breath as he studied the photos in detail. Finally, he put them down and looked at Rosie. "Yep, pretty much sums up the way all our victims were killed. To the letter, in fact. Okay, now to blow your mind."

"Hang on a sec – and put something over these. I wanna get a refill."

Scott looked at her for a second, then moved one of the manila folders over the photos as Rosie signaled to Shirley.

Rosie turned toward Scott. "You want another of those?"

Quickly, he placed his hand over the top of his cup. "Nah, I'm good, thanks. I'll be headbutting walls if I'm not careful." He chuckled.

Rosie nodded, though the remark seemed a little odd to her. However, she dismissed it as one of his idioms, since he seemed like quite a straight up guy and not a beat-the-truth-outta-the-suspect kind of agent.

Shirley approached with her warming smile and refilled Rosie's cup, then wrinkled her nose in a playful manner and wandered off once more in search of other customers in need.

Scott moved the folder away from the photos, then stared at Rosie in silence for a moment, as though creating intentional suspense.

It worked. Rosie found herself leaning forward toward him.

"So, Rosie, let me ask you something. What do you think of horror movies?"

She jerked back a little, the question catching her off guard. Her eyes darted. "Ummm, love 'em, I guess, although it takes a lot to scare me these days."

"Yeah?" Scott gave a sly smile. "Well, hold on to that thought."

He had her; gripped, filled with intrigue. The way he doled out information in a teasing manner had Rosie thinking he must be quite the storyteller. She sat upright.

Scott continued. "Okay. From the information we received from one of the experts we consulted, we believe that this is some form of satanic ritual, possibly to summon the Devil himself.

Rosie nodded.

Scott reached into a folder and retrieved a piece of paper containing diagrams of the very same symbols found on the bodies of Rosie's victims. He pointed to each one in turn. "Each of these symbols represents one of eighteen portal codes, as our guy called them."

"One of eighteen?" she said, her brow raised.

He nodded. "One of eighteen, yeah. Within my investigation, we have twelve victims all killed within a certain area, in sixes, within weeks of each other It is our belief that our perp intends to kill a total of eighteen in blocks of six. In short, three blocks of six."

Rosie inhaled an excited breath. "Six, six, six. The number of the beast."

Scott grinned. "Exactly. Getting kinda creepy, huh?"

"That's putting it mildly, yeah."

He flicked his eyebrows at her. "Indeed. So, taking your case into consideration, this is a solid hypothesis, since we now have victims thirteen, fourteen and fifteen."

Rosie nodded slowly in agreement.

"And I think the last three will occur this week."

She frowned.

"The timescale of the previous victims would support that, and I just have this feeling that we are hurtling toward a conclusion here."

"Fair enough." Rosie said with a nod.

Scott finished off his coffee, wincing slightly at the cold, yet strong-flavored liquid then continued.

"Now, for the longest time, I couldn't for the life of me figure out what connected the victims. It was like the most random serial killings ever and in circumstances such as those, catching the perp is damn near impossible."

"Why do I feel a 'but' coming," Rosie said.

He smiled and held up a finger. "But. Eventually I stumbled across a link. And when I say stumbled, I *mean* stumbled.

"Come on then – spill. Whaddaya got?"

"Horror movies!"

Rosie's brow furrowed and she leant back in her seat. "Horror movies? You're fucking with me, right?"

"Nope. Horror movies. Having interviewed each of the victims' friends, the one thing that kept coming up was them saying it was kind of ironic that the way in which the victims were murdered would've fitted into the sort of horror movies they were into."

"Get the fuck outta here," she blurted.

"Rosie, you gotta understand I was bone dry on leads. In some cases, it took four or five interviews with different friends before they started to feed me info that they most likely thought was insignificant at first. But I just kept digging. On its own, that info wouldn't have been much of a trigger, but—"

"Well, of course," she said, interrupting him. "A lot of people like horror movies. That doesn't make them targets for serial killers."

"Exactly," he said, his excitement growing. "But it was a piece of information that kept cropping up, and so I joined the dots."

"Okay." She sat back in her chair. "They all part of one particular group or website or something?"

"No," he replied, his eyebrows raised. He threw his hands into the air. "None of them knew each other, or rolled in the same circles, or had any cause to have bumped into one another."

"Soooo?" Rosie's eyes widened

"So, at first I thought that maybe they had been to the same conventions or such, but there was nothing to that in either." He shrugged.

Rosie sighed. "So where's this going? Seems you're back to square one."

"Not exactly," he replied, leaning forward. "The other significant piece of info I gained from each of the vics' friends was that they were all very difficult to scare. They had watched so many movies, to the point of fanaticism, that they had built up a tolerance and were seeking more extreme forms of horror to view."

"Figures. Okay then, a specialist horror site or store connection? C'mon, there's gotta be something."

He smirked and shook his head. "If only it was that easy. But I'm afraid I drew another blank."

"For fuck's sake, Denver. What *do* you have?"

He looked at her as though to ask, *Why are you not getting this?* and shook his head. "Don't you see? Each of the victims had an unnatural tolerance to horror."

"So?" she said, exasperation setting in.

He seemed to deflate for a moment. "Check your photos again, the ones showing their faces."

She stared at him for a few seconds and then, reluctantly, resumed studying the macabre shots. She sorted through the pictures and fanned out the ones showing the victims' faces.

"Look at the terror on their faces," Scott said, pointing to the pictures.

"Oh, for the love of God, Denver. Forget their tolerance to horror movies. If someone was doing that to you for real…" She shook her head. "This proves nothing."

Scott held up a hand. "Hold on. Our post-mortems indicated that each victim was dead before any of these acts were carried out. Were yours the same?"

She frowned, then nodded slowly.

"So that proves the victims were terrorized beyond belief before they were killed."

"Again, Scott. It proves nothing. Anybody would have been terrified in that scenario. Movies are not real life, and some serial killers get a kick out of not making it quick."

He nodded. "Agreed. But there's more. Most also displayed signs of long-term fear and terror, but it appears their deaths occurred very quickly following their disappearances, so there was nothing to suggest long-term torture."

"How do you know that?" Rosie asked. She was getting a little tired of the guessing games.

Scott pulled out another file from his folder and laid it in front of her. "Toxicology showed an increase in the production of hormones associated with acute and prolonged fear." He pointed to a chart. "Cortisone, epinephrine, et cetera, et cetera, plus signs of swift weight loss. In a few of the victims we found they had lost as much as forty pounds in something like two weeks."

Rosie glanced at him sharply. "Really?"

"Yeah. Supported by photographs prior to their time of death. And not only that; in a couple of cases they showed signs of rapid aging, as though they had been subjected to such an insane amount of fear each day that it had caused the production of gray hair before their years." He pulled another photograph from his folder. "Look at this. A twenty-eight-year-old woman with a full head of white hair. Now check this photo. Two weeks before, that hair was jet black. Have your investigations not provided similar results?"

"Not in the white hair department, no – you're ahead of us there. We will have tox data, but I highly doubt we will have made a 'fear' connection. Look at how they were murdered: our lab guys would have assumed it was par for the course."

He nodded. "As did ours, initially."

"Well, I'll make sure we check those links now. So what's the bottom line?"

"It is my belief that the victims are subjected to a significant state of fear and terror, most prolonged, a couple short-lived, but all hyper-intensive. This is most likely undertaken within their own environment. Then, when they are at an optimum point for whatever is the next part of the perp's plan, they are murdered in the manner shown here. However, what I still cannot explain is *how* they are selected."

Rosie sighed. "Aaaaand, we're back to square one."

Scott pursed his lips and shrugged. "There is simply no known link between these people other than the fact of their love for horror movies and initial tolerance to terror." He slumped back in his seat. "From here, it's baffling me, Rosie, and I hate that. I fucking hate that."

She glanced at him sharply and smiled. She hadn't heard him swear during these past couple of hours, and hearing him do so made her feel a little happier about him. He was normal after all. Maybe not as foul-mouthed as her, but still.

He sighed and sat forward again. "But we have a bigger problem than my lack of knowledge—"

"Victims sixteen, seventeen and eighteen," she said. "And this week, according to your hunch." She raised her eyebrows.

"Exactly. And furthermore, I believe that once he has those, he's gone and will never surface again. Satanic rituals followed to the letter tend to have an ultimate conclusion, never to be repeated."

Rosie took a deep breath and frowned. "One thing bothers me, though. You say eighteen victims, yeah? But he's killed way more than that, with all the guys in my team."

Scott nodded. "Sure, but not in this way. And actually, that fact right there is cementing my hypothesis about how this guy operates. For his ritual to be compete, it is about how the victims are prepared and then killed."

Rosie eyed the horrifying pictures once again. "Jesus, Scott. We gotta catch this guy, and fast."

He looked at the photos and nodded. "Okay, now something from you. How did you manage to find him? That is something of great interest to me."

She laughed weakly. "Well, I wouldn't get too excited about our detective prowess on that score. We received a tip-off that the person of interest was holed up at a particular address and would definitely be there at a particular time. Intel confidence was high since the email mentioned certain case points not made public."

"You deduce it was your guy, fucking with you?"

"That thought played into our planning, of course, but we had to act upon it."

He nodded a little. "Email, huh? You trace the IP?"

"Yeah, but it was some internet café in New York City. NYPD. are still onto it for us, but nothing useful seems to be coming from that lead. Not as yet, anyways."

He nodded once more. "So what else ya got? Even if you feel it's insignificant. That also goes for anything post-incident."

She frowned "Post-incident? What do you mean by that?"

"I mean, have you experienced anything weird since that night?"

Rosie's mind drifted for a few seconds, thinking back to what Dr. Williams had said to her during her back-to-work interview:

"If I sign you off as fit for duty Rosie, it's imperative that you let me know immediately if you experience any post-traumatic psychological relapses that would affect your ability to do your job. Is that understood, detective sergeant?"

'Loud and clear, doc.'

Rosie pressed her lips together. "Nope. Nothing at all that I can think of." She wasn't going to let anything get her taken off this case.

He sighed. "Okay then. Well, let's just review your incident footage and all the case files with a fine-toothed comb, and see if we can't find something."

She nodded as he started to gather his evidence and put it away.

Scott rubbed his forehead, then his eye. "I'll have my guys at the New York office liaise with NYPD. and get some more eyes on the café and surrounding cameras etc." He finished putting his info into his briefcase and shut it, clicking the latches into place. "Each of my batch of six were in a three-mile radius of one another, so a good start would be the perp's house where, well… y'know." His tone and demeanor took a slightly more somber turn.

Rosie nodded thoughtfully. "Yeah. I know."

He pressed his lips together and stood. "Okay then. Shall we get to it? You can fill me in on the details on the ride over to the house."

Rosie paused for a few moments. Was she ready to go back to *that* house so soon?

"Now?" She asked.

He shrugged, his eyes wide, then nodded.

Rosie sighed, then gathered the rest of her things as she shuffled out of her seat. "Yeah. Okay. Let's go."

9

Wednesday 7th November 2012, 11.45am.

Rosie's feet wouldn't move. She wanted them to, but they wouldn't respond; she clenched and unclenched her fists and closed her eyes, attempting to get them obey her commands but instead they resisted, as though they knew something she didn't. A premonition of things to come from which, perhaps, they were trying to protect her.

The last time she had stood in front of this door, she'd experienced much the same fear and trepidation, but on that occasion she'd felt a sliver of control, aware of her ability to handle the situation, given the inordinate amount of aggressive entries into dangerous environments she had performed previously. Not only that, Larry had been there, and she'd felt reassured despite the terror that had gripped her; he had kept her from spiraling into a useless mess. But today, having walked the path that led to the house, there was something different, something new about the creeping terror that had begun to rise within her. Staring at the door had provoked new levels of fear that had her mind swimming and as though that fear was telling her, *Do not go in there, just walk away and forget everything. You do not need to see. You do not need to know. Trust me, I'm here to help!*

She realized she had been holding her breath for several seconds, and exhaled; it must have been noticeable, as Scott took hold of her elbow gently.

"You okay, Rosie?" he asked with a frown, stepping in front of her so that he blocked her view of the house.

She flinched, the interaction snapping her out of her trance. She offered Scott a nervous smile and laugh. "Yeah. Yeah, I'm fine. Just… y'know, it's strange, looking at the place. It's just… strange." She looked at the house again. "Seems much less ominous during the day, though." She glanced at him again, then looked away, knowing that her nervous smile had betrayed her lie.

Scott stared at her for a few seconds, then turned to eye the house.

In fairness to Rosie, Scott had begun to have a sense of what she must be feeling, such was the oppressive atmosphere that seemed to spill out from the foreboding property. Of course, he could not know exactly what she had experienced, nor could he fully appreciate the extent of her own internalized anxiety resulting from that event, but from her trepidation it was clear that she was suffering from high anxiety, despite the target of their investigation being long gone. Yes, he could feel it. The house simply felt… wrong.

"Look," Scott said, "just… take your time, yeah? It was clearly a traumatic experience and we will go in only when you are ready. This is not an uncommon occurrence when such post-traumatic stress has—"

Rosie pushed past him, reminding her body who was in charge. It was as though Scott's words had cut through her fear and anxiety to speak directly to the detective within her; the rational side, the cop who got things done, who faced the unknown with all the training under her belt and a burning desire to confront things which most people could not. She strode up to the door confidently, took hold of the yellow-and-black *Police – Do Not Cross* tape and, with both hands, pulled it apart forcefully relishing the symbolism of the action. Reaching into her pocket, she drew out a key, slid it into the lock and turned it. Then she paused, her eyes closed, breath held. After a few seconds, she opened them, exhaled sharply, then pushed the door.

Her mind jolted as darkness flooded around her. She looked to her right, realizing she now had her back to the wall at the side of the door, her weapon raised, and she could see Larry on the opposite side, looking at her as automatic gunfire rang out and screams came from within the house. Then Larry spoke.

"Okay. Okay. Listen, we're cops, yeah? If we are going in, we're doing this right."

Her mind raced, and she shook her head, attempting to sift through her thoughts and make sense of it all. She knew that what she was seeing couldn't be happening, that it must be a memory of that night, but the images were so clear and so stark that it dazed her. She closed her eyes, then snapped them back open as Larry spoke once more.

"It'll be okay, Rosie, trust me. We go on three."

Her lips began to tremble, and her body followed suit and tears beaded the corners of her eyes. She knew full well what was about to happen.

Despite having that knowledge, the suddenness of Larry being ripped through the doorway by an unseen force made her jump and scream – as did the hands that gripped her shoulders.

Scott shook her hard, only making her screams intensify. She waved her hands in front of her face.

"Rosie!" he said, trying to bring her back into the moment. Then he shook her again and shouted, "HENDRICKS!"

The second, more forceful action seemed to do the trick: Rosie ceased her screaming and flailing and looked directly into his eyes.

"You're okay, you're okay. It's not that night. You are here with me. It's not that night, Hendricks, it's just a post-traumatic reaction. You're okay. It's okay."

She batted his hands away and breathed out hard, pushing herself away from the wall and forcing Scott to take a step back that almost made him stumble.

"You're okay, Rosie," he repeated, but she turned away from him and strode through the door.

She was angry, and she was confused. The vividness of the memory had been almost too much to bear, but the thought of Scott Denver now questioning her ability to remain rational was even more overwhelming than the terror she had just faced. She could *not* be taken off this case. She owed too much to Larry, and to herself, to let her irrational behavior be her undoing. She ran her fingers through her hair angrily, then turned to face Scott, only now aware she was in the hallway of the house. She stared at him for a moment, expecting him to say something more to her and then looked away.

Scott held up his hands, approaching her as though she were a dangerous predator.

"Look, Rosie, whatever it was that just happened to you just now, it's fine. It's okay. You may have gotten your body back on the beat, but your mind may take more time. What took place that night has been burned into your psyche for good, and it had to manifest itself at some point. What just happened was a healthy thing and, trust me, it stays right here with you and I and goes no further."

She turned back to and stared at him again. His words offered her more comfort than she could possibly explain to him. She realized that he got it; he understood and, in that moment, her trust for Special Agent Scott Denver elevated to a much higher level. She had no reason to trust him as she now did, given she had only just met him, but every fiber of her cop body was telling her that this guy was alright, that he was on the level. Her mouth opened to say something but he shook his head at her, lowering his hands.

"Don't. There's no need. You tell me right now that you are okay and good to go, and I will accept that."

She smiled slightly and nodded.

He smiled back, her gesture clear and without obfuscation. "Good. Right, then. We will figure this thing out and you can find some peace for your guys. You need to be on the job and working, so let's get to it and do what we do best."

She took a deep breath and closed her eyes for the briefest moment, then reopened them and began to look around.

Scott moved to one wall and flicked the light switch. Nothing.

"Power's off," he said with a sigh. "Goddammit, don't they know we are still conducting an investigation?"

Rosie shrugged as she continued to survey the entrance hall. "Power company doesn't care. It's all money to them. Just doing their jobs, I guess."

Scott nodded and, in the gloom, he spied the vast amount of bullet holes peppering the walls and floor. "Jesus," he said, moving closer to a grouping in the wall, "some goddamn firefight in here. How the hell did they miss the guy?"

Rosie turned to look at him. "Well, that's what we're here to find out. Pete and Martin and the guys back at the station said they have been through this place thoroughly and come up with zilch. I trust them implicitly, but we need to be better. There's something here – I can feel it – and we need to find it, whatever it is." She walked to the wood panels under the staircase and poked a finger into one of the bullet holes. "Listen, I'm gonna walk the place a little on my own, see if something doesn't pop out. At least that way we ain't covering the same ground and looking at the same shit."

Scott nodded. "Fair enough. You take downstairs, I'll go up?"

She looked around for a couple of seconds, then agreed and headed toward the living room. As she passed through the archway leading into the living space, an inexplicable feeling hit her and she raised a hand to the center of her chest and took a deep breath, steadying herself against the decorative wood of the archway's framework. As quickly as it had arrived, the sensation disappeared and she exhaled forcibly, blinking a few times as she regained her composure, her head swimming in disorientation. *Get a grip, Rosie,* she told herself. *This is all in your head, a psychological reaction to trauma. You know this. Don't let it get the better of you.*

She rolled her neck until it cricked, the tension having tightened up the muscles. She glanced toward the large window and then to the Chesterfield armchair directly opposite it. It looked old and tatty, as though it had been rescued from a street corner, its light-brown color interspersed with cracks that spread everywhere upon its surface like the veins of a leaf. She noted that the room was peculiarly devoid of any other furniture: no settee or side cabinet, or even any pictures on the walls. There was nothing above the fireplace; none of the usual ornaments resting on the mantel, and no mirror. Nothing. It was as though the only purpose the room served was for somebody to sit in that armchair and stare out of the window.

It was then she noticed that there were no curtains, only a mucky gray net covering the full length of the window. She thought back to the night when Gerry had been adamant that he could see the perp in his thermals through the wall and then the window, and the even crazier part where he insisted it had suddenly become two men, not just one. She jabbed her hands onto her hips and returned her gaze to the armchair, then moved closer to it. "What the hell were you looking at, Gerry?" she whispered to herself.

An ethereal voice calling her name from behind her made Rosie slap her hand to her weapon and spin around, but she could not see anyone. She held her breath and cocked an ear toward where she had thought the sound had originated, but could not detect any movement or noises. She began to move forward when the same ghostly voice spoke again from behind her, in the direction of the armchair. She froze. She began to hyperventilate and could see her breath, the temperature in the room having dropped rapidly. She closed her eyes and tears formed as her breathing began to race even more, and her heart thumped in her chest. She felt goosebumps ripple all over her arms and then she succumbed to a shudder as cold air brushed against her neck, accentuating the creeping terror that had started to move through her. Trying to introduce some semblance of control over the situation and to bolster her courage, she asked, "Who's there? West

Babylon P.D. – identify yourself." She was hoping that calling out the challenge in such a loud and forceful manner would gain Scott's attention upstairs, and that he would come charging down and into position as backup. But nothing answered, instead there was only silence.

Still, something was there – she knew it. She was so certain of its presence that she could almost feel it breathing down the back of her neck – then she wondered if indeed the sensation was actually exactly that; that somehow, someone or something had been hiding in the room all along and had waited for the opportune moment, distracting her with a thrown voice to the other side of the room, then creeping from the shadows, most likely from behind the armchair, to sneak up on her, waiting to attack. The rational portion of her brain told her that such a thing was impossible, that there could be no way she would fail to spy someone hiding behind the chair, that it could not conceal a human other than maybe a small child. But rationality had left the building and she was operating on the fantastical, her mind racing through every eventuality, every dark scenario. Her lips trembled, her hand even more so as it rested on the butt of her gun. She closed her eyes once more as the voice echoed from behind her. This time she knew she had not gotten it wrong; that it was who she thought it was.

Standing behind Rosie was the severely mutilated and grinning corpse of Larry blood dripping from his chin and patting onto the floor. He shuffled toward her a couple of steps, his movement slow and uneven and dragging a leg and then reached out to her. "Rosie. It's me, Rosie. It's Larry."

"No," she said. Her tightly closed eyes spilled tears, then she shook her head. "Larry's dead. Who… who is that?" Still she could not open her eyes, and still she could not turn around. Had psychosis taken hold? Was she indeed losing her mind? She didn't know what would be worse; to turn around and see Larry there, or not to see him. Either presented serious issues that she did not want to deal with. She took a deep breath, trying to force herself to open her eyes and turn around, but her terror was winning and all she could do was shake her head. "Who is that?" she repeated.

"You know who it is," the sly, ghostly voice said, echoing around the room. "Turn around."

The last two words repeated many times, whispering and bouncing within her mind. She shook her head once more, feeling an onset of hysterical bawling rise within her and threatening to take over, and it took all she had not to succumb to it.

"No!" she stated, "It's impossible. You're..." She paused, pondering the word she was about to say, then snapped her eyes open. "He's dead." She had found something within her, enough courage to open her eyes, but not yet enough to turn and face whatever it was her mind had her believing was behind her. She took in another sharp breath as the ghostly voice of Larry spoke once again.

"I know, but here I am anyway, and my pain is beautiful, my torture exquisite – and soon you will be allowed to join me down there, in his wonderful world, where he will make you purr with ecstasy in your own, personal horror."

She felt that she was on the verge of hyperventilating again, so erratic had her breathing become. She could now smell the decay, the stench of death and disease. It stung her nostrils but still she could not move, not even to raise a hand to cover her nose to stop the nauseous, overpowering odor. She gagged, feeling violently sick, but nothing came.

Larry's grotesque corpse continued to reach out to Rosie, but had stopped advancing, its head cocked to one side and its grin spread even wider, even more unnatural. He chuckled.

"This isn't real," she said, shaking her head again. "It's all in my head. This is just my grief. I won't turn around. I won't turn around and make it real or give it life. I won't." She closed her eyes tight and began to count to ten. She had not even passed four when Larry's chuckling snapped her eyes open.

"I'm still heeeeere," he said, his voice sly, playful, and mocking. "Let me show you something."

He shuffled forward a few more steps toward her and reached around her head with his mangled and bloodied hand, then tapped her forehead.

Rosie's eyes shut tight again.

They opened almost immediately.

She was outside the house again but for reasons she could not comprehend, she was watching herself while participating in the vision at the same time, her back to the wall, her weapon drawn and held in front of her. The sound of gunfire and screams filled the night air once more; this was the night of the incident. She looked to her right to see Larry. She saw his mouth open and close; everything was happening in slow motion and she knew what he was saying though the words were inaudible: *"It'll be okay, Rosie, trust me. We go on three."* He started to count just as the unseen force ripped him through the door. Rosie screamed. Then the same force hoisted her into the air and into the house, time returning to its normal speed.

She landed upon the floor of the hallway with a painful thud, dropping her gun, which slid away out of reach. She looked up to see a pair of S.W.A.T. team members scream and open fire and she curled up into a fetal position beneath them, her arms covering her head as empty bullet casings rained down all around her. She flinched as, one by one, each team member was lifted into the air and their bodies were broken and mangled in front of her. The sickening sound of bones breaking and muscle and tissue snapping made her feel physically sick. She cried with terror as they were sent hurtling through the air and crunching into walls, their bloodied bodies sliding down unnaturally, leaving behind a wet, sticky red trace of their life force rather than dropping quickly.

Her attention snapped to another team member as he was dragged up the stairs, his screams punctuated by the thud of his helmet as it banged against each step. Then, without warning, the carnage ceased and the room became deathly silent; Rosie almost cried out at the sudden loss of sound. Breathing rapidly and sharply, she took her arms from around her head and looked around.

Her gun was nowhere to be seen, but she did spy a carbine rifle dropped by one of the team members, so she scrambled to pick it up. As she went to examine its chamber, the weapon cracked and split in half and she dropped it with a scream of surprise. Frantically, she searched the room for another weapon, painfully aware that her breathing was so erratic she was shouting with every breath. She fought hard to bring it under control. Her face creased in anguish as hopelessness began to seep in. She might have succumbed to it if it were not for her squeezing her eyes shut and letting out a murderous scream, then beating the floor with a closed fist.

"Get yourself together, Hendricks," she shouted at the top of her lungs, then began to haul herself to her feet. She froze midway through rising, as a deep and guttural laugh drifted from the blackness of the living room before her. It seemed to draw closer but Rosie heard no footsteps. The chuckle came again; she could tell it was only few feet away, right at the edge of the darkness, and she felt she might relieve herself right there on the floor. The laughter stopped, replaced by a heavy breathing. It locked her in position, bent double and staring into the blackness.

And then the oddest sensation took over: of wanting to see what was at the edge of her vision, almost needing to. To finally know what waited there, ready to stream into the meagre light of the hallway.

The breathing continued to grow louder, and Rosie began to cry as an ethereal face began to materialize within the darkness. It was pure white and seemed to be grinning. Her body became wracked with total and utter terror, and she screamed harder than she had ever done in her entire life as a hand grabbed her shoulder. Responding to sheer instinct, she spun around and raised her gun.

She was back in the present, in the living room, in the daytime, and facing a startled Special Agent Denver, whose hands were raised, his eyes wide and his mouth open.

"Whoa! What the fuck, Hendricks? It's me, Scott... Special Agent Denver. Get a hold of yourself. It's me! For fuck's sake, it's me!"

Rosie took a sharp breath and then quickly lowered her firearm to her side. "Oh my God. Jesus, Denver, I'm sorry, I'm sorry. Jesus Christ." She exhaled hard, then spun around and checked the room. "Did you see him? Did you see him, Scott?"

Lowering his hands slowly, his brow furrowed, Scott took a step toward her. "See who?"

"The guy... the voice... the..." She exhaled hard again and dropped to a kneeling position. "Fuck me, Denver. I think I'm losing it. I don't think I can be on this case." She began to cry.

Scott reached down to comfort her. "Who did you see, Rosie? Tell me."

She bent over further and put her head between her knees, still sobbing. "I didn't really see anyone."

Scott stared at her for a couple of seconds then pulled his hand back and frowned.

She sniffed. "Larry. My dead partner, Larry, just spoke to me and I could feel him in the room with me." She lifted her face and wiped her eyes with the back of her hand that was still holding the gun. "Then there was a face... or *almost* a face. I dunno. Jesus Christ!"

Placing his hands on her upper arms, Scott hoisted her up to a standing position and looked directly into her face. "Tell me everything. Tell me *exactly* what happened."

She stared at him for a few moments, then shook her head and pushed past him. "I need to get out of this fucking house. Right now," she said as she hurried for the door with Scott calling after her.

She burst out into the noon sun, though the air had an October chill, and placed her hands on top of her head as she staggered down the path.

"Rosie. Wait. Stop," Scott said as he chased after her. "Detective!" he shouted, causing her to stop and turn to face him.

"What?" she responded, her hands slapping down by her sides in frustration. "What do you want to hear, huh? That I'm fucking whack-a-doodle, batshit, out of my mind crazy?"

He held up both hands in a placating gesture. "I don't think you're batshit crazy, but I do want you to tell me what just happened; what you just experienced."

She let out a nervous laugh and turned away, her fingers pressed to her brow, then turned sharply back. "Everything? Okay. Well let's start with the fact I just heard my dead partner speak to me and tell me he was in Hell or some shit. Then he touched me, right here," she tapped a finger against her forehead, "and I was back outside the house on that night, and then both saw myself and felt myself dragged inside like I was watching some insane movie and participating in it at the same time." She began to pace up and down frantically, one hand placed against her forehead while letting out laughter that bordered on lunacy. "Then, I heard something that scared the shit out of me coming from the living room."

"Like what?" Scott asked softly, attempting to calm her a little. "What did you hear?"

It worked: Rosie stopped pacing and looked at him, her hand still pressed against her forehead. She stared at him for a couple of seconds before continuing. "I don't know what it was, but even though it sounded like him, it sure as hell wasn't Larry, that's for certain." She dropped her hand and took a deep breath. "I was standing in the hallway, looking into the dark room, and…" She paused, trying to recollect an image within her mind. "Something was in there. And it wasn't anything that you would want to see, that much I know."

Scott nodded a couple of times and stared at her without saying a word.

She became angry once again. "Oh, fuck you, Denver. Fuck you. You think I'm crazy." She gave another exaggerated, maniacal laugh with a hand placed to her forehead that she then ran through her hair. "Maybe I am fucking crazy. Maybe I have fucking lost it."

He placed a calming hand on her shoulder. "I don't think you're crazy at all. But I do think you've been subjected to something."

She stared at him, unsure of where he was going with this.

"I need to call Forensics to organize another sweep through the house."

"A sweep-through. For what?"

He pulled out his phone. "When I interviewed the previous victims' friends, they all reported that the victims had been having hallucinations and seeing crazy things, terrible and terrifying things." With a few jabs at the screen, he entered the passlock code and it clicked. "It is my belief that they, and you, may have been subjected to some sort of substance that could cause this reaction, these hallucinations. I believe it is one of the methods our perp uses to manipulate and terrify his victims."

Her head tilted back in her surprise at his information. "What? Why the hell didn't you mention this before?"

He began to say something, then stopped. He glanced away for a second before Rosie's irritated slight raising of her arms signaling, she is waiting for a response brought his attention back to her. "I wasn't sure, but I was waiting to see if you, as a control subject and as someone who may have been previously exposed, would have another reaction – even if it was a long-shot. And I didn't want to taint the control element by giving you a pre-conceived notion."

She stared at him. "Oh, thank you; thank you very fucking much. Really appreciate being your guinea pig." She turned away with her hands onto her hips, cursing under her breath. She turned back to face him. "You think I'm tweaking?"

He offered a faint smile. "Not exactly. I'm getting Forensics down here to do a more thorough check.

Rosie flapped her arms in frustration. "But we had people in here already. Surely it would have affected them."

"Yeah, I guess, but this time I want them to be alert and checking for any signs of gaseous substances, or perhaps something on the walls or furniture. Did you touch anything?"

She looked at the ground, her eyebrows knitted as she tried desperately to remember. She shook her head. "No. No, I don't think so." She gave a small sigh. "But this isn't the first time this has happened since… well, since then. I heard Larry calling my name in my apartment a short while back."

Scott tapped his phone a couple of times, then raised it to his ear, nodding at her. "This is why I asked earlier about any post-incident occurrences. Maybe it's something the guy made you eat unwittingly or injected you with, but the timeframe for that would be crazy."

Rosie nodded. "Yeah. How could something remain in my system for that long?"

Scott shrugged. "Beats me, but it's something we gotta—" He cut his sentence short and turned away as someone answered his call. "Yeah, hey. This is Special Agent Denver, and I'm at the incident house on America Avenue with Detective Sergeant Hendricks. I need a Forensics team down here ASAP." He turned back to face the house and stuck a finger in his ear to block out the sound of a car as it drove by behind him. "And you will need to liaise with the C.D.C. and have one of their guys either accompany or advise you, as we may need their help identifying any suspicious or unknown substances."

Rosie stared at him as he nodded and vocalized agreement. It was clear the person on the other end was asking questions and probably taking notes.

"Yeah, that's correct," Scott continued. "I want you to check for external toxicological substances and I am also gonna need bloods running on detective Hendricks. Yes… okay. Understood. Thank you. Goodbye." He hung up and put his phone back into his jacket pocket, then made his way back to Rosie. "We'll get to the bottom of this, Rosie, I promise. This is a good start to a lead, I think."

She nodded, then looked back at the house, chewing her bottom lip. Scott patted her on the back and made his way back to the car. She took another deep breath, nodded again, and turned to follow him.

From an upstairs window and behind a net curtain, a figure stood watching Rosie and Scott walk away; and he grinned.

10

Wednesday 7th November 2012, 10.30pm.

Rosie rubbed her eyes with her thumbs while leaning on her desk. She gave a long yawn that made her eyes water and forced her to rub them once more. She was tired, dead tired; the events of the day had taken more out of her than she had initially realized. She was no stranger to long nights at her desk in front of her laptop, as she was now; combing through mountains of evidence and information, trying to decipher the nature of whatever problem or mystery she happened to be working on at the time. Full to the brim with coffee, enough to keep anybody going, and consumed in such amounts that there was the regular and welcome distraction of drawing straws with her colleagues to see whose turn it would be to go and refill the jugs – a game she often lost and one she was convinced that Pete, Martin and Gary cheated at.

She looked around, suddenly remembering she hadn't yet seen her friend, Gary Cross, in the office, although she wasn't surprised. He hadn't really been the same since the death of his little boy, Jacob, and having been being pulled back from the brink of alcoholism and depression by his old partner, Paul Keenan, he had opted for a more solitary approach to his work and kept himself busy in the field. Plus, he seemed to have an uncanny knack for getting a lot of his paperwork done away from his desk, something Rosie envied a great deal. She smiled inwardly; she really liked Gary, one of the best detectives she had ever met. And a bit of a fox, too.

She shook her head. *Goddammit, Rosie. Get your goddamn head back in the game.* She sat up straight and rewound the footage from Gerry's thermal camera on her laptop. There was something she was missing – she just knew it, and she was certain Gerry and Donny's thermals were

72

the key. There must be something that she had overlooked, the smallest bit of information. Despite Scott's explanation, and his subsequent requirement for a deeper look into the forensics angle to the case, the events surrounding Gerry and Donny were so fantastical that she wasn't sure it could be explained away by 'a weird gas.' Not to mention the way in which their bodies were discovered. The thought of it gave her the willies; she shuddered.

She was in the process of freezing the picture at the point Gerry noted he could see the guy through the wall (Rosie still could not) when Scott approached her desk.

"That was the lab," he said, finishing a call and slipping his cellphone back into his jacket pocket. "Your bloods are clean. They would like to run some more tests, but I said that can wait until later." He leaned over to study the image on the screen. "Sniper footage again, huh?" Rosie glanced up at him and he frowned. "Sheesh. Those rings around your eyes get any darker and I'm gonna have to call you Rosie panda." He chuckled.

Rosie stared at him for a moment then cocked her head to one side briefly. "I hope your singing's up to scratch, Denver, cos your comedy ain't worth fucking shit." She gave a wry smile.

He huffed a laugh. "Nah, 'fraid not. Singing's even worse, if you can believe that." He smiled.

"Oh, I can. Believe me, Denver, I can." She turned back to the screen; the smile now spread across her face.

He laughed under his breath and nodded.

Scott liked Rosie and had started to get more of a measure of the woman since their coffee meeting that morning. Having spent the best part of the day with her in the precinct following the incident at the target house, they had been sifting through evidence, and he had been able to formulate a better picture; not being able to do so before then had bugged him a great deal. Now, having enjoyed a little more banter with her, he knew he was right – that she was a straight-as-an-arrow, down-to-earth kinda gal who most likely got on better with guys than she did girls, and without doubt could give as good as she got. He had enjoyed their time together today, despite her earlier trouble within the house, and was hoping he might get to know her a little better when they had this case nailed.

Scott's eyes widened as he realized what kind of thoughts he was having. *Get back on the clock, Denver,* he told himself. *Shit like that is unprofessional and you should know better.* He became uncomfortably aware that he hadn't said anything for a few seconds and was half-expecting Rosie to comment on it. When she didn't, he cleared his throat gently. "You nudged any more info out of the footage?"

She sighed and shook her head. "Nahh. And I still can't understand why Gerry said he could see the guy through the wall, or window even. Thermal imaging just doesn't work in that way."

Scott nodded. "Right. Thermal imaging can only detect heat as it radiates off an object. So yeah, there's just no way. And windows tend to block infrared energy waves, soooo…"

Rosie glanced up at him, her mouth downturned. She nodded. "Very good, Special Agent Denver. Nice to know you're not just a pretty face." She realized immediately the dumbness of what she had just said, and felt liquid magma of shame spread up her neck and into her cheeks. She looked down at her desk, her eyes darting back and forth.

Scott saw immediately how uncomfortable she had made herself feel (and him, too, for that matter) and so he decided to be the chivalrous gent. He knocked her playfully with his elbow. "Ahhh, you're not so bad yourself, ya know, Hendricks. For a dude, that is."

She laughed breathily. "Dick," she said as she turned back to the laptop screen, grateful for the 'out' he had provided. "But as I said, I just don't get what Gerry was on about. But," she held up a finger, "what you said before got me thinking. Perhaps whatever substance this guy is using could be deployed airborne, somehow?" She glanced at Scott again.

He pursed his lips and nodded. "Could be. Perhaps, yeah."

She tapped the screen with her pen. "I then started thinking about how Gerry and Donny were found a half mile away in the street. Maybe they came into contact with this substance, freaked out, fell to their deaths off the roof, and then our perp moved the bodies after he had killed everyone in the van. Y'know, to really fuck with us?"

Scott took a deep, contemplative breath and tilted his head to one side. "Maybe. I guess there's more likelihood of that explanation than one that suggests they were hurled a half mile away from their rooftops. But – and I don't mean to throw a spanner in the works here – those roofs weren't so high that a fall from them would without doubt kill two guys. Maybe one, by a freak broken neck, but two guys in the same way?" He frowned. "Plus, their wounds were more suggestive of injuries sustained from falls from much greater heights, and at a much higher velocity." He sat on the edge of her desk, then laid a hand on her shoulder. "I'm sorry, buddy. Just doing the job, y'know."

Rosie gave an angry growl and ran her hands over her head. "Goddammit. What the fuck went on in that house and with that bust? It's driving me mad."

Scott removed his hand and stood up. "Yep. Well. When we solve that piece of the puzzle, we'll be well on our way, I reckon." He looked at his watch. "Look, it's getting kinda late. Let's call it a night and get back to it bright 'n' early tomorrow morning, yeah? We have nothing more to go on for today, and we're gonna start going around in fierce circles if we're not careful and miss something. Unfortunately, what will be, will be, and our guy will still be here tomorrow."

Rosie stared at the screen. "Yeah. That's what worries me."

11

Wednesday 7th November 2012, 11.45pm.

Removing the towel from around her head, Rosie leant forward, shaking her hair. She placed the towel on her lap and frizzed her dark-brown locks between her fingers, then grabbed the towel again and rubbed her head vigorously once more. Sitting up quickly and throwing her hair back, she mussed through it a final time with her fingers, then threw the towel onto the table beside her laptop, which displayed a still image from Gerry's thermal camera. She stared at the image for a few seconds and scratched her nose and then the back of her head, as once more her mind wrestled with all the information from Gerry's and Donny's feeds. But, as had become the norm as she studied the evidence, her thoughts once more came up blank. The whole thing had really started to bother her.

She grabbed the mouse and moved the timeline slider all the way to the left again to watch the footage for what felt like the hundredth time. She leaned toward the screen, desperate to spot something she had missed previously, begging her mind to impart a revelation that would move her along at breakneck speed and bring her closer to not only understanding the mysterious elements surrounding the case, but to also determine the location of the killer himself. Once more, she watched the footage all the way through and gave a deep sigh as she prepared to repeat the process. Looking down at the table briefly, she scratched her forehead; taking hot showers always left her skin a little dry and itchy. She considered heading back to the bathroom to grab more moisturizer, but then decided against it, her need to keep working far outweighing something as minor as an uncomfortable skin sensation.

"Goddammit, Gerry. What am I missing here? What the hell were you seeing?" She bit her bottom lip. She then brought her legs up and sat cross-legged on her chair and pressed play.

Her eyes darted, checking each corner of the screen to see if anything new presented itself, or to spy something she had missed. She reached for her cup of hot chocolate laced with whipped cream – a guilty pleasure that had made the crossing from childhood to adulthood – then stopped, her hand hovering over the table, close to the mug. She listened as Gerry stated defiantly that he could see the guy through the wall, and her mouth opened wide, then her eyes too. She could now see the form of a man, seemingly sitting in what must be where the Chesterfield armchair was situated. The figure was brilliant white, as a thermal camera would display. Her head shook and her mouth remained open. Her hand trembled as she drew it back and she sat back in her chair as the white figure stood, looked to his right, then left, then straight ahead, and began walking forward and to his right, toward the window. Once again, Gerry's voice cut through, stating that there were now two of them – two guys – and almost on cue, another figure of a man, that looked identical in shape and stature to the first, peeled away from behind the other figure and moved toward the archway that led into the living room. Rosie's hand shot to her mouth as more figures appeared from behind both men, and then more from behind those figures, replicating like dividing cells within an organism – more and more, until the screen became overwhelmed with white. Then they stopped duplicating themselves, and the head of each figure looked toward her in unison.

Terrified, her hand shot toward the laptop screen and snapped it shut. Then her hand returned to her lips, trembling, and she pushed her seat back and stood up. She stared at the laptop for a few seconds, before walking toward her kitchen area. Then she stopped and began pacing up and down in the space between the living room and kitchen.

"What the fuck, Hendricks?" she said. She often addressed herself in the third person when trying to figure things out, another little habit that had transitioned from her childhood to adult life. She did this particularly in times of stress, and Lord knew she'd had many of those in the past, having to listen to her warring parents. She put her thumb into her mouth and began to nibble at it – another of her tics, again brought on initially by moments of anxiety, enduring the spiky atmosphere of her childhood home. She hadn't had a particularly terrible childhood, but it hadn't been great either. At some point when she was around seven years old, her parents had become increasingly hostile toward one another and the arguments could explode from any little, seemingly innocuous, thing. Like most children, Rosie had wondered if it had been her fault; if they had been arguing about her. Her father had perished in a fire just over a year later, and the amount of growing up she had to do to help her mother, who become almost catatonic, had seen her dismiss all such childish notions and had changed her outlook on life. But here she was again, acting like that scared and confused seven-year-old, nibbling her thumb, and trying to make sense of a situation that had gotten away from her. Was Scott right? Was a substance that she had contracted from the perp still running rampant in her system, or was something infinitely more sinister at play – supernatural, even?

She spun on her heels, chastising herself. *Don't be ridiculous, Rosie. There is a rational explanation for everything that happened and that you have seen. A rational explanation. A rational one.* She repeated the words over and over, but a part of her struggled against it.

After the death of her father she had been sensitive to experiences and happenings that she could not explain and that her young mind, (although maturing at an unintended rate) had latched onto; it turning to fantastical, supernatural possibilities rather than logical ones. But soon after, she dismissed any such notions as pure juvenile folly, and pushed them deep down, never to be considered again, moving on to young-adult stage much earlier than her friends and peers. Now, however, those feelings came flooding back, the same irrationality that she had experienced all those years ago. Somewhere deep inside she knew that what she was witnessing and living through was a true supernatural experience and not some form of gas intended to induce horrific nightmares.

She ceased her pacing up and down. "Okay, Rosie Hendricks," she said, "you're not a child anymore and there's no need to let your mind spook you. There has to be a logical explanation for what you have just witnessed. Get a drink of water, get some sleep, and check your sanity in the morning. That's an order, woman." She saluted, then broke into an erratic laugh. "Oh my God, I'm giving myself orders now," she said, jamming her fingers into her hair and sweeping it back. "You've definitely lost it, Hendricks. Definitely." She shook her head, then trudged into the kitchen where she ran a glass of water, took a sip, and went to bed.

From a corner of the kitchen the demon stood watching as it had most nights since Rosie had returned to her apartment from the hospital. He smiled, one that spread across his chalky-white face that was half covered with his long, jet-black, hair; baring horrific, crooked, sharp teeth, while piercing red eyes studied her every movement. His tongue licked his blood-red lips. It was time for him to have some real fun with her.

12

Thursday 8th November 2012, 01.05am.

Rosie's eyes snapped open, and she glanced to her right at the sound of scratching at her bedroom door. Her breathing stalled and her eyes widened as grunts and sniffs followed the scratching; the sound so deep and powerful that it could only come from a large animal. It intensified, and Rosie closed her eyes and began to count to ten, hoping she was in the moments between being asleep and awake. Her mind ran rampant, fear pushing to the forefront as a new and terrifying sound made her eyes open sharply: the violent rattling of the door handle.

She took a deep breath and held it, tears beading in her eyes as terror engulfed and paralyzed her. Then she shut her eyes tight, causing the droplets to spill down her cheeks and roll onto her neck. She exhaled sharply, suddenly aware that she had been holding her breath for too long, then pulled the top of her sheets up over her mouth and toward her eyes as the animal sounds at her door grew even louder and more frenetic. She felt as though she had regressed to childhood. to become that scared young girl watching horror movies with her friends, too scared to look and instead using a blanket thrust over her nose as the ultimate form of protection.

She was shaking, as though she were outside in the cold night air and freezing to death, the adrenaline coursing through her veins trying to prepare the body for what might come next. Then, for inexplicable reasons, her fear vanished, replaced by another emotion, one that was familiar and that she had relied upon for many of her adult years: bravery. She became angry with herself for allowing the idiocy of terror to take hold. Fear was not always the enemy. Fear could be a good thing; a motivator and instigator of common sense, but over the last few days she had allowed it to take a firmer grip of her than she liked, and she had now finally reached snapping point. She became determined to face that fear and drive it back into the shadows. She remembered who, and more importantly, *what* she was – a cop. So, through gritted teeth and with a grunt, she threw off her bed sheets and scrambled out of bed, quickly opening the drawer of the bedside table that held her gun. Grabbing the firearm, she drew back the top-slide and checked that a round was chambered – it was – and then moved with the professional purpose of a law enforcement officer to her bedroom door. She placed her back against the wall to the side of the door handle. Taking a few deep breaths, she steeled herself to deal with whoever, or whatever, was on the other side of the door, still rattling the handle – though the grunting and sniffing had now ceased.

"West Babylon P.D., armed officer," she shouted. "Whoever is on the other side of the door, take a step back, lie face down on the ground with your hands on your head, and await further instructions."

The handle ceased its rattling, something that caused her to take a sharp breath and hold it. She closed her eyes; she knew this was it and she needed to act, had to hope that whoever was on the other side of the door had been compelled to comply with her instructions and was now in the position she had demanded and that she wasn't about to enter into a situation beyond her control. She mouthed a silent prayer, opened her eyes then reached down to the handle, turned and pulled it. Her weapon in front of her, she moved swiftly through the doorway and into the room. "West Babylon P.D., get down on the ground with your hands on your head."

But the room was devoid of life. There was no person, and no animal, to her great relief.

Her ears detected a sound toward her front door, so she moved with purpose toward it. As she cleared the hallway, she looked to her left, past the kitchen, to see the front door complete the final inch of closing and then clicked into place.

"West Babylon P.D.," she repeated, loud and forcefully, "stay where you are and put your hands on your head." She moved to the apartment door and yanked it open. Taking control in this manner and doing her job, she felt more confidence and bravery flooding back into her, and she strode into the corridor aggressively, her weapon raised and never straying from the direction in which she was facing.

Again, there was nothing there – but just like in her apartment, the door at the end of the corridor closed and clicked into place; something had definitely just gone through it. She was happier now that she was convinced it was a human being and not an animal; chasing humans was part of her job description.

She lowered her weapon, still holding it in two hands, and ran the fifteen feet to the door, then flattened her back against the wall and raised her weapon to one side of her head. With her left hand, she reached down and turned the handle, then forced the door open and moved swiftly into the stairwell, immediately checking her corners and the floor above. She saw nothing and so, holding her breath, she stood perfectly still and cocked an ear, listening for sounds to determine which direction her quarry had fled.

There! Below! The sound of footsteps hurrying down.

Once again, she shouted a challenge, then set off in pursuit, her legs working overtime as she skittered down the stairs, sometimes two at a time. Below, she heard the familiar sound of the front door to the apartment block opening, its draught trim scraping along the floor, and it then starting to close slowly on its hydraulic safety arm. Once more she challenged whoever it was to stop.

Reaching the door just before it had completed its closing arc, Rosie pulled it open again and ran out into the cold, November air, suddenly aware she was in her pajamas and barefoot. She kept her weapon raised and held out in front of her, her breath billowing like steam as she fought to bring her breathing under control. There was nobody there and she was certain that nobody could have had time to complete the sixty yards from door to entrance gate leading to the apartment block, nor was there anywhere to hide in the meagre foliage alongside the pathway.

Then she froze in terror at the scraping noise of the lobby door behind her, which signaled it was being opened. Had she missed the person she had been chasing, somehow? Perhaps they had not run out the door, instead pushing it and then quickly retreating to the mailboxes under the stairs. Had her haste been her undoing? *My God – are they armed?* She closed her eyes, annoyed at herself for making such a rookie mistake and not checking the entire entrance hall before bounding out of the front door. She prepared to turn around quickly to command whoever it was to get down on the ground – but then her fear returned in massive quantities.

A maniacal, creepy voice whispered from behind her, "Roooosieeeee," rooting her to the spot, and she felt hands slip over her shoulders and grip her. She just had enough time to glance down at them to see they were horribly clawed and disfigured, before they yanked her backward and everything went black.

Thirteen

Rosie grunted as she landed with a hard thud onto a wooden floor and her head rocked back and cracked against the hard surface. She threw her hands over her head and covered her face as S.W.A.T. team members around her unloaded their automatic weapons in random directions and seemingly at nothing, their screams piercing the barrage of noise, somehow louder than the gunfire itself. Their vocalized terror seemed right at her ears, as though their owners' mouths directly beside her. She peeked through the shield formed by her arm to see one team member being dragged up the stairs, his terrified cries destroying any last semblance of calm or bravery that might have lingered within her. Then, abruptly, the room became deathly quiet, and she was alone, the sudden silence more terrifying than the preceding cataclysm of noise.

Slowly, she lowered her arms to confirm that she was once more back in the house on that fateful night. This time she knew beyond any reasonable doubt that she wasn't dreaming; that she was somehow reliving the event. Her mind did its best to tell her that it was impossible, that she could not be, but a part of her shunned that notion. She was where she was; it was real, and it was happening. She looked down to see that she was still dressed in pajamas. She pinched her arm, hard, and felt the fierce sting, then saw the redness. The act reinforced the reality of the situation.

Her eyes darted around, looking for her gun, aware she was no longer holding it. But she couldn't see it; instead, she spied a S.W.A.T. team member's carbine, and she scrambled across the floor to grab it. She then leapt to her feet and drew back the charging handle to check a round was chambered, then released it. She had begun to raise the weapon when it split in two without warning, as though something ultra-sharp yet invisible had sliced through it. It dropped to the ground. She staggered back a few steps and it took all of her strength and character to not burst into tears and crouch into a ball, to bury her head into her knees and will herself away from that place, to be anywhere other than where she was right now.

Her attention snapped to a deep, guttural croaking sound that drifted toward her from the pitch black of the living room. Her breathing became shallow and erratic and she clenched and unclenched her hands, feeling the sweatiness of her palms, then rubbed her fingers, all the while maintaining focus into the darkness. She wet her tongue, suddenly aware that her mouth was dry, and tried to swallow but found it difficult, such was the aridness at the back of her throat. She took a couple of steps backward, toward the staircase, as the croaking turned to laughter and drew closer. She wanted to run, to bolt out of the door, but somehow she knew that such a thing would not be possible and that on the other side of the front door there would be nothing: an empty void. She didn't know how that knowledge came to be in her mind, but sensed it was correct all the same. It made her dizzy, forcing her to blink a few times, and she swayed upon her feet.

Rosie screamed and stumbled backward into the paneled wood of the staircase as a horrific-looking man streamed from the darkness of the living room. His feet hovered above the floor, pointing straight down, and his clawed hands hung at his sides. His jet-black, straggly hair covered part of his face and a terrifying grin spread across his features. He had blood-red lips and jagged, sharp teeth. His red eyes bored into her, filling her with even greater terror.

"Jesus Christ," she said, almost screaming the words as he drew closer to her, towering above her, and she held her hands up to her face.

"Jesus Christ?" the demon said, his head cocked to one side. Then he roared with laughter. "JESUS CHRIST!" His laughter abated, and he adopted a menacing expression. "Fuck him. He cannot help you, the pathetic worm." He laughed again and leaned down to her, his grin somehow spreading even wider, and becoming even more unnatural. "You really have no idea what you are dealing with here, do you?" He chuckled, slightly more reserved than his previous laughter. "Funny how you would turn to that fucker despite the struggles you have with your beliefs. Did you learn that from your mother?"

She stared at the creature – she understood he was not human – and her breathing stuttered as she lowered her arms slowly from protecting her face. She was almost too terrified to think clearly, let alone speak, but she knew she must, and that she could; not because she wanted to but because whatever it was in front of her was going to allow it. That thought scared her the most: the level of control this thing possessed over her. She tried to wet the inside of her mouth, swallowing hard and feeling the sticky dryness as her tongue stuck to the roof of her mouth. She nodded slightly as she tried again, this time clearing her throat. She took another deep breath, teeth gritted, then asked, "Who… who are you?"

The demon smiled, wicked and unnerving. "Oh… all in good time, my child, all in good time. But first, I would rather we talked about your mother. We can discuss who I am later, when we have become much closer, and more intimate, friends."

His smile became a wide and toothy grin and his clawed hands moved to either side of his mouth and his fingers rippled at the skin. His bloodshot eyes opened wide, glimpsed through his straggly hair. Devilish glee danced within them. Rosie didn't think there was any more room for terror within her, but she was wrong. This was just about the most horrific thing she had ever seen, and she felt as though she might relieve herself at any moment. The demon bent over, an unnatural movement as he still hovered above the ground, and leaned in even closer, his nose almost touching hers. She turned aside, recoiling in horror at the sight of him and the awfulness of his breath, stale like decaying flesh.

He stared at her, his grin growing ever wider.

The demon loved her reaction – every single bit of it, for this was his calling, the music that he danced to – the terror of humans – and he wanted more: to gorge on her fear, to taste it in his mouth.

He chuckled again. "There's something you should know about your mother. Your precious, pious mother, the deeply religious whore that she was."

Despite the fear that gripped her so tightly, and ignoring his closeness, Rosie shot a glance at him that burned with hatred and anger.

The demon's head flew backward and he let rip with laughter again. "Oh, so it does possess spunk. Good. Maybe this one will offer some form of entertaining challenge after all, and not be a pathetic piece of useless piss that cowers and shakes before me like a shitting dog, as all the others did." He floated backward and inhaled deeply through his nose, still grinning. "Yes. Your mother was very much into her religion, wasn't she? Or was it that religion was very much into her?"

He laughed again, deep, guttural, and demonic, and Rosie's brow furrowed and her eyes narrowed.

"The priest who was always around... a family friend, or something much, much more, perhaps?" Slowly, his grin returned. "Yes, always there, even when your father wasn't. Or should I say, especially when your father wasn't."

More demonic chuckling.

"They were very, *very* close, your mother and the priest." He licked his lips with a long, slender, pointed tongue that curled back on itself. "Oh yes, he was very much into her, he was into her all the time, fucking her brains out, in fact. And you – the stupid little girl who never suspected a thing – you just played with your little dollies and dreamed of a princess's life far, far away." He smiled as he floated closer to her, then reached down with a clawed hand from which she recoiled. "But who could really blame you? You were such a delicate little flower, wholly unsure of the world and how it worked – much as you are right now."

"You're lying," Rosie said, still edging away from his touch and quivering. "My mother wasn't like that. She was a good woman."

The demon scoffed. "Oh, but you're wrong; she *was* like that. Exactly like that. Think back and I am sure you will remember how excited she would become when the doorbell would ring and she knew that it was him standing behind it, waiting to come in, glee in his eyes, sending you off to play and then taking your mother to her room where he would stick things in her. Oh yes, she could not get enough of that priest." He roared with laughter once more.

Somehow, Rosie managed to overcome her fear and replace it with anger. From deep within her, an untrammelled aggression erupted and she lunged at him, her fingers raised like claws, ready to dig her nails into his face.

But the demon was not only too fast but also much too strong, and he lunged at her quicker than she could at him. He gripped her hard underneath her arms, digging his fingers in, and crunched her into the wall with thunderous force.

She screamed at the pain, then gurgled as the creature grabbed her by the throat and lifted her into the air. Her hands shot to his single one and wrapped around it, attempting to prize it off while her feet kicked ineffectually. He squeezed hard, and she retched and panicked even more, clawing at his hand in a desperate attempt to remove it.

He drew his face closer to hers. "Your mother was fucking the priest, and furthermore, your father knew about it."

Tears beaded in Rosie's eyes She beat at his hand and tried to shake her head, desperate to find any way to draw in breath and fill her lungs. To her immense relief, the creature relaxed his grip, allowing her enough space to breathe, and she inhaled as much as she possibly could, tears spilling down her cheeks.

He then dropped her to the ground; she fell with a grunt and began to cough and retch, one hand massaging her throat.

The demon descended gently to the ground, then turned and walked away from her a little. "So now let us talk about your father." His tone was insincere, even mocking. He glanced back at her over his shoulder as she gathered herself, rubbing her throat. "Your fine, brave, upstanding policeman father who died saving a poor, sweet and helpless old woman from a blazing fire, thus making you the cop you are today. Or at least, so you thought. But your father was not the virtuous soul that you hold so dear in your thoughts. No, he was something much more malevolent."

Still on her knees and trying to collect herself, Rosie looked up at him in disgust. "My father was a hero," she said, the words coarse-sounding due to the damage her throat had taken. "You have no right to speak of him like that."

The demon threw back his head and laughed with gusto. "Wrong. WRONG, WRONG, WRONG. Your father was no hero and he did *not* save an old woman from a fire. He burned to death in a pitiful whorehouse next door to where the fire started." He sneered at her. "A place in which he had spent a lot of time, after finding out about your mother. The truth was kept from you to…" He smiled and looked up into the air, his arms dancing around his head as though he were conducting an orchestra. "To protect you." Slowly, he lowered his gaze back to her.

Rosie began to sob. She lowered her head and shook it. The things he was saying… none of it was true – it couldn't be true, she knew, for despite her parents' faults, such deceptions and awful actions were not possible. Whatever this damn creature was that tormented her, it was lying, trying to unseat her mind and her resolve, and she could not allow that to happen. She *would* not. She shook her head again. "No. That's not true. It's bullshit."

"Oh, it is true, child. And furthermore, he had a favorite. Marcia. A sweet girl. A young girl. And do you know how old she was, hmm? Do you know just how tender and succulent Marcia was? Fifteen. A mere fifteen years old." He chuckled again. "What does that say about your dear, wonderful daddy now, huh? Oh, how he belongs with us in the pits of Hell. How he loves his torture that my brethren inflict upon him daily. How delightful, how delicious, how... righteous it is." The demon threw his head back and roared with laughter, then turned away and began to walk back to the darkness of the living room.

"THAT'S A LIE!" Rosie screamed at the top of her voice. "That's a fucking dirty lie." She began to sob. "Why are you doing this? Why are you doing this to me?"

"A lie? Child, these are not lies. I am merely opening your eyes to the truth, to the reality of your past." He turned around to face her fully. "But this is nothing. I am simply preparing you for what is to come. Darkness. Sweet, beautiful darkness. Magnifique," he said, and kissed his fingers. "And with that darkness... pain. Pain so sublime the screams of you and your kind will fuel us for an eternity."

She looked up at him as he opened his mouth into a terrifying grin once more, baring his teeth. When he lunged at her, a terrified scream erupted from her and she raised her arms in front of her face.

And just as it had when she had been grabbed outside the apartment building, everything went black.

89

14

Thursday 8th November 2012, 01.11am.

She screamed and scrabbled to reach an upright position, arms flailing violently around her head, trying to fight off the terrible creature that had leapt onto her. Then, realizing nothing was attacking or molesting her, she opened her eyes to discover that she was back in her bedroom, and in bed. She began to pant, her breathing fast and erratic. She felt at her pajama shirt: it was dripping wet from sweat and stuck to her skin. She brushed her hair back, as it was matted to her head, irritating her. As the onslaught of tears arrived, she grabbed at her shirt and knotted it as she pushed it into her chest.

She cried. Hard. Like she had as a child when ripped out of sleep by night terrors, only her mother able to help; her soft, warm, and loving lips pressed gently against Rosie's forehead, arms wrapped around her and smothering her into her mother's bosom. Her calm and soothing words whispering into Rosie's ear that, before she knew it, chased the horrors of the dream away and made her feel safe and warm. How she wanted that now; how she needed her mom to be there and make everything better. But that was not possible. Her mother was dead and no amount of tears, now or in the past, would change that.

Kicking off the covers, Rosie swung her feet out of bed and pressed her face into her hands. She stared into the blackness behind her eyelids, then took a deep breath, composed herself, running her hands through her hair and then down to her chin, her mouth open a little. She glanced to her right, grabbed her cellphone, and flicked through the contacts until she found Scott's number that he had given her a few hours earlier, before they left the office for the night. Selecting it, she closed her eyes and rolled her neck. The horrifying event had taken its toll, filling her with anxiety and stiffness and leaving her feeling broken. She knew it hadn't been a dream; it had been real and had really happened. She couldn't explain it, nor did she want to try right now, but the familiar feelings had returned – her sensitivity to paranormal and unexplained events that had persisted through childhood – and she didn't intend to ignore them. Every fiber of her being was screaming at her to believe the encounter, to trust in her gut reaction, which was something she always did. She was not going to betray the one person she could rely on: herself.

She resigned herself to the phone going go to voice message when Scott's gruff and tired voice answered. "Umm, hello? Rosie? It's one-twenty in the morning. Is everything okay?"

"No. No, it is not."

"Okay. Okay. Err, what's going on? Can I help?"

She was about to speak when Scott continued.

"Sorry, that was a dumb question. Of course I can help or you wouldn't have called. I'm not fully awake yet. It was a long day."

"It's okay," she replied, "and yeah, you can help. I need to see you. I'm coming to you."

Scott was about to respond, but the line had gone dead. He sat upright then yawned and threw his phone onto the bed. "Okay, she's coming here. Fine." He glanced around the motel room and nodded, satisfied that it was acceptable enough for a visitor, as neatness and tidiness were high in his priorities in life. He swung his feet out of bed, stood and began to get dressed.

****

When Scott opened the door, he stepped back a little and frowned. "Jesus, Hendricks; you're either super-tired or super-stressed, and I can't decide which."

"Both," she said as she pushed past him, failing to make eye contact.

He nodded as he closed the door, then turned to face her and his eyes narrowed as she sat on his bed and put her head in her hands. Quickly, he moved closer to kneel in front of her as she began to sob. He wasn't sure what to do. Should he put an arm around her? No. *That wouldn't be professional*, he thought. To his relief, she answered the question for him, grabbing hold and embracing him, burying her head into his shoulder and then his neck. His eyes darted and his hands hovered over her back, not sure if he should commit and wrap them around her to bring her in tight.

Rosie sensed his trepidation and his clear discomfort and backed away slowly. "Sorry," she said then sniffed. She wiped her nose, then the corner of her eye. "Kinda just needed that."

He wanted to assure her everything was fine, but couldn't seem to find the words, so he just shook and then nodded his head. After a few seconds, and with an embarrassed sigh, he sat next to her. "Well, that was a weird couple of minutes." He smiled and gave a small chuckle. "Care to fill me in on why we just went through all that awkwardness?"

She glanced at him, thinking about what she wanted to say, how she wanted to tell him all that had happened. On the drive over, she had been absolutely certain how she would explain the incident and all the strange goings-on that had preceded it. How she would explain convincingly that it wasn't some sort of gas or substance she had been exposed to, as Scott had suggested, but, in fact, a true supernatural experience. However, as she sat on the bed, staring at and fiddling with her hands, she began to doubt her own sanity. Everything she had planned to tell him now seemed like total and utter madness. She was convinced he would stare at her, mouth agape, considering whether to call for assistance to haul her off to the loony bin.

She was about to speak when he put his fingers gently under her chin and raised her head a little, his eyes narrowed.

"How the hell did this happen?"

She stared back at him and frowned.

"Your neck," he said, turning her head left and right, making her wince. "Jeez, Rosie, how the hell did this happen?"

Her hand went to her neck and she winced again upon touching it. She stood quickly and moved to a tall standing mirror situated next to the door, and checked her neck. She took a sharp breath. How had she not noticed the finger marks and bruises until now? More importantly, how had she not felt them? She ran her fingers over them and again reeled at the pain.

"What the hell is going on, Rosie?" Scott asked, approaching her and frowning. "Who did that to you?"

She swallowed hard, suddenly aware that her throat was dry. "Got any coffee, or better still… bourbon?" She gave a giddy, erratic laugh. "Fuck it, both, in fact."

He studied her for a moment before conceding, "Got coffee, no booze, though – sorry." He crossed to a side cabinet that housed cups and saucers, a kettle and various hot beverage ingredients, switched on the kettle, then turned to face her. "Rosie. Please. What the hell is going on?"

"I was attacked," she said, the instant he finished asking his question, almost interrupting him.

"Attacked?" His eyes widened. He moved briskly over to her. "Attacked by who? My God – are you okay?"

She took a deep breath and moved back to sit on the bed. "I don't know who he is, but I know he has been haunting me since I came home from hospital – and not only that, I am ninety-nine-point-nine percent certain he is the guy we are looking for."

Scott stared at her, puzzling over her choice of word: *haunted*. He had no words to offer and nothing came to mind that would express his bafflement. But a strong part of him knew everything she had just said, and what she was inevitably about to tell him, was true. He couldn't explain it, but he knew it to be the case. Ever since the start of the investigation, the sheer level of inexplicable events and behaviors surrounding the victims had him scratching his head, trying hard to come up with explanations that *didn't* point to the supernatural. But he knew, deep down, that the next five minutes were going to allay any notions to the contrary in that sense, and he would have to deal with the consequences of accepting such things to be true head-on. He went to the dresser, grabbed a chair, then dragged it across the room so that it directly faced Rosie. He sat down and took a deep breath, then rested his forefinger on his lips, his thumb under his chin, and leaned toward her.

"Go on then," he said, "tell me everything, and don't leave out any detail, no matter how small or crazy it seems."

Rosie glanced up from her fiddling fingers and scoffed. "It's usually me saying that line to my witnesses."

He offered her a slightly embarrassed smile and looked down for a moment before looking back at her. "I hear ya, detective. Look, we will figure this out."

"You'll think I'm mad!"

"A few weeks ago? Maybe. But honestly, now, and looking at you… Well, I am willing to accept anything, as the case is just about as weird as it can be, and something's telling me that you're right, we're not looking for a super-gas. I haven't known you long at all, but I am willing to bet my career that you haven't done that to yourself." He pointed to her neck. "So start at the beginning and tell all."

She looked at him sharply, her eyes glistening, betraying gratefulness that her mouth could not verbalize; gratefulness at not having to spend an hour trying to convince the F.B.I. agent that she wasn't mental, that she wasn't making it all up. She wanted to hold him again and pull him close and breathe in the smell of his neck, to thank him with more than just words for the fact that he believed her, and more importantly, he believed *in* her. She chastised herself, annoyed at allowing her professionalism to slip and for her to succumb to his allure. This wasn't the right time to be thinking anything of that nature, and there was no room for desire. She had been drawn into something of great importance, and that carried significant weight – that much she knew – so she had to bury any notions of entanglement and do the one thing she knew how to do above all else: be an officer of the law and put a stop to whatever was about to occur.

"Thank you," she said, smiling at him, reaching out and gently cupping his hands in hers. She told herself it would be the last semblance of intimacy between them. She sat back and more upright than she had been.

When the kettle clicked off they both looked at it, but then ignored it. What Rosie was about to say was, without doubt, more important.

She looked back at him with a half-smile. "I don't know who or what he is, but this is a power, an entity that is beyond our understanding. I have felt his presence for a number of weeks but had put it down to my grief, or more accurately paranoia brought on by grief, and I'd been scared to say anything about it – terrified, even – in case it compromised my ability to be back on the streets. But tonight," she half-laughed through her nose, "well… tonight was different, and so very, very intense. I knew – positively *knew* – that I wasn't in a dream or imagining it – it was too vivid for that."

Scott nodded. "Okay. What happened? How did it start?"

"As it did before. I was brought out of sleep knowing that something was very wrong; acutely aware of it. And I heard something scratching and sniffing at my door."

Scott sat back in the chair, his eyes wide.

"Yeah, exactly," she said, raising her eyebrows. "At first, my mind said, 'Dream: you're still dreaming,' but I soon knew that wasn't the case. It seems so silly, so obvious that we can distinguish between dream and reality, but when you're in such an event, within your dreamscape, it can sometimes take weird markers to tell you that you are dreaming. But this time, this… experience simply screamed at me: *this is happening, Rosie.*" She looked up and laughed, aware of how idiotic it all sounded.

Scott inhaled deeply through his nose. "Don't. Don't do that. It doesn't sound mad at all. Tell it as you see it – or more importantly, how you *felt* it, as it may lead to and unlock information that we would normally overlook, especially when not investigating in a manner that would befit Mulder and Scully."

She chuckled. "Oh my God – an X-Files fan, huh?" She laughed again. "I am so glad you don't think I'm fucking nuts."

He smiled. "Hey! What kind of an F.B.I. agent would I be if I didn't like the X-Files? If I'm being honest, I'm excited to be in one."

Rosie's smile waned. "I wouldn't be, Scott. Because something tells me this is no joke, no game. Something is about to happen that is unbelievably important. I can't explain it." She stared ahead and her eyes darted as though seeking something. "But it feels, I dunno, like something that will affect the entire world." She sighed. "Am I even making sense right now?"

He nodded. "Of course. Like I said, don't leave out any details. Please, go on."

Rosie stared at him for a couple of seconds before continuing. "Okay, so I grabbed my firearm, issued a challenge, and went to see who was there. But there was nothing, no one. I ran into the living room and saw the front door to my apartment closing, so gave chase to what I thought was an intruder. I chased him down the stairwell and outside but, again, there was no one there. And that's when it happened."

He cocked his head to one side and sat forward.

"Hands grabbed me from behind and dragged me backward. I thought I was going to land in the hallway of the bottom floor of the building. But when I looked up, I was back in the target house. And it was *that* night."

Scott sat up straight again, eyes wide, mouth agape. "You were back experiencing the night of the arrest attempt?"

"Yeah," she said with a slight nod, "but it wasn't the same. I still don't have total recall on that night's events, but even though the first part felt real again—"

Scott held up a hand. "Whoa, wait. What do you mean, the first part? And also: *again?*"

She nodded, realizing he was missing vital information. "When we went to the house yesterday afternoon and I inexplicably pulled my weapon on you, I had the exact same experience, frame-for-frame, as last night, right up until the part you pulled me out of it. And I mean the *exact* same. Being dragged into the house, landing on the floor with the team around me engaging an unseen enemy as it tore through them. And I gotta tell you, Scott, it's so intense, the sensation of being there, knowing it is one hundred percent real, that it is not a dream state or hallucination. On the first occasion, you managed to bring me out just before he got to me. I could sense him moving through the darkness toward me, and I was so grateful that you got me out. But last night, there was no one to help and it was as though the dial had been turned up to eleven. He came at me out of the blackness of the living room and attacked me. I could feel every ounce of pain he inflicted upon me. I could smell his awful breath when he grabbed me by the throat and leaned into me. It had made me want to be violently sick. But then he told me things – *awful* things – about my folks. Lies. Horrible lies." Her hands went to her forehead.

Scott leaned forward again. "It's okay, Rosie. You can do this. We will work through this together. What was it he told you? What did he say?"

She ran her hands back, drawing her hair into a ponytail. She sat up and took a deep breath, and wiped her eyes in turn. "Look, my family wasn't perfect, okay? We had our share of troubles." She paused as Scott nodded sympathetically, her eyes wandering, her mouth opening and closing, searching for the right words. "And I know I was young, but I wasn't stupid. I knew my mother and father weren't in the best of marriages, that there had been an undercurrent of falling out, of arguing and not wanting to even be in the same room; but they always made the effort around me. And some of the things this guy was saying… some of those things were too much, too disgusting to even be considered true." She closed her eyes and shook her head, then opened them again and stared at the floor.

The problem was that despite her flat denial of anything the creature had said, her mind – her cop mind – refused to let go of the information, and had begun to piece incidents and events together, no matter how innocuous they had seemed at the time. The vile and evil things the creature had said had flicked a switch within her mind and she was struggling to turn it off. But she couldn't succumb to those thoughts; she wouldn't allow herself to. No matter how bad it had gotten between her mother and father, or how much they had fallen out before her father's death, they could not have been capable of the things *he* had said. They just couldn't.

She took a moment to organize her thoughts, to get back on track and continue detailing what had happened. "My dad was a cop, and a damn good one at that. But – the same old, tired story – the job had affected his marriage in too many negative ways, and he and my mother were at the end of their tethers. But, my dad being my dad, he had been a hero right to the end, having responded to a call after a fire broke out, having fortuitously been in the area. His colleagues said he managed to save a number of lives before the smoke overcame him and the fire took him."

Scott's eyes narrowed. "My God, that's awful. I am so sorry."

She appreciated his genuine and heartfelt sincerity. She pursed her lips and nodded. She half-smiled as a memory danced through her mind. "It's funny, but despite how they had grown so far apart, the news had hit my mother in the worst possible way." Rosie glanced at Scott. "She had a vicious mental breakdown and eventually took her own life, not being able to live with…" She paused, looking up briefly. "Well, with the guilt… I guess."

The guilt of the death of your dad in a fire, and unreconciled differences, or of something else? a voice in her head said. She tried to push the thought away but it was doing it again, her brain doing its cop thing, cynically addressing the evidence and actively looking for holes in previous information. She hated it right now and didn't want to listen, so she turned her attention back to Scott.

"But the things this guy said were completely out of order. That my dad had died next door to where the fire had started and then spread – that he was in a brothel, with a fifteen-year-old girl."

Scott sat back sharply and took his hand from his chin.

"Yeah, exactly," she said. Her eyebrows rose and her tone became sharp. "But the problem is, my mind is spinning in all directions. I thought I saw a girl in my room the other day, even heard her voice; so what the hell does that mean?" She stared at Scott for a few seconds. His face was locked in a display of absorbing unbelievable information. She continued, "And not only that, he said that my mother had been knocking off the local priest, which had led my dad to the bottle and into that sort of depravity."

Scott blew air through his lips and shook his head.

Rosie laughed nervously. "I don't know what to do, Scott. I feel like I am losing my fucking mind."

Scott was about to say something, but then he jumped up and scrambled backward, knocking the chair over in the process and almost falling to the floor himself. "Jesus H. Christ, what the fuck is that?"

Rosie spun around on the bed and followed Scott's lead, leaping off the bed and moving to his side as she saw what had terrified him.

The demon stood in a corner of the room, arms spread wide, grinning; its mouth displaying his horrible teeth and his eyes pure white, as though they had rolled all the way into the back of his head. He opened his mouth even wider, to such a degree it should not have been able to talk; yet it did.

"His time will soon be at hand. We are close to our most glorious victory, and once the child is gone, once He has her, there will be nothing left to save humanity and we will shriek with delight as you tear each other apart and join us for eternity where your pain will be the music to which we will dance and celebrate." He cackled and then roared with laughter.

The sound was despicable – evil and rotten – and it hurt Rosie and Scott's ears, making them thrust their hands over them and push tight to try to block out the sound. But it was everywhere. It shook the room like an earthquake and worse still they could feel it within them. And each of them pushed their ears tighter, in the vain hope the action would stop it worming its way into their brains where it would bury itself and remain and torture them forever.

Rosie screamed, terrified and helpless. She shut her eyes so tight she could feel the pressure on her eyeballs. She wanted to be away, anywhere other than where she was at that moment, far away from this horrifying and debilitating nightmare. As the raging laughter reached a crescendo, and as she thought she could not take a single second more and that her mind would explode, it stopped, and the room fell into an unnerving silence save for Scott's muted groaning.

Slowly, and through panting breath, Rosie opened her eyes. The demon had disappeared. Her attention snapped to Scott as he rose to a standing position, having been forced to crouch on the floor.

"What the actual fuck was that?" he said, his hands on his head and tugging at his hair. "What the actual fuck!"

15

Thursday 8th November 2012, 01.05am.
Rosie glanced at Scott, nibbling the skin of her thumb as he prowled the length of the hotel room, his head bowed slightly and rubbing his chin periodically. He had been pacing up and down for a couple of minutes, mumbling to himself and shaking his head, trying to come to terms with what had just happened. Given the shock he had just endured, she had decided to leave him to it, to allow him to process the supernatural event. But she was feeling scared and helpless too, and she needed to start processing this herself. For her, that meant dialogue and discussion.

"So, whadda we do about this?" she asked, pulling him out of his agitated musings.

He stopped and stared at her for a few seconds then shook his head. "Honestly, I have no clue." He jabbed his hands onto his hips and stared at the floor for a moment, then looked back up at her. "But I might know someone who could help."

Rosie became attentive and stopped biting her thumb. She shuffled to the edge of the bed to signal her piqued interest. "You do? Who?"

He walked over and sat beside her. Looking at her briefly, he then turned his attention to the door for so long that it prompted Rosie to call his name. He smiled and shook his head. "Sorry. Mind's working overtime." He looked down at his hands and fiddled with them, then looked back up. "After I investigated the eighth victim, her mom, who was obviously distraught, said she 'knew who had done this' – she knew who had done that terrible thing to her daughter."

99

"Okay," Rosie said, bringing one leg up and tucking it under the other.

Scott sighed. "You have to understand, she was in a terrible way, inconsolable, and I didn't think anything she said had made any sense."

Rosie nodded. "Understandable."

He paused, gathering his thoughts. "Okay, so, she told me that a devil stalked her child, that it had stalked and eventually killed her." He raised his eyebrows and made an exasperated sound. "Of course, I read between the lines and determined what she actually meant in her heightened state of distress was that whoever had done that to her daughter, whoever that man was, she regarded him as a devil; that's how she saw him." He paused again, then shook his head. "But every time I said to her: 'I promise, I will catch the person responsible for that heinous crime,' she kept insisting that I had it wrong, that it was a devil and not a person, that it was no man. I even said to her that we could not be sure it was a man, and she shook her head at me and replied, 'I know, it's a devil.'"

Rosie offered a tired smile, despite the fact that nothing about this situation, or Scott's story, was funny. It was a mere expression of how right the woman had been, given the information they now possessed.

"So what did you do?"

"Well," he said, with a deep breath, raising his shoulders, "Mrs Mubatu then got up and rummaged through a drawer and gave me a card." He looked around the room, then reached to the bedside table for his wallet. Opening the bulky item, he rifled through a host of small business cards to find the one he wanted and handed it to Rosie. "This card, in fact."

She took it from him and looked at the front, turned it over, then flipped it over again. "Doctor Wilson Kalisha, Witch Doctor." She looked up. "A few days ago, I would have died laughing and thought you were off your noodle, Denver. Not so much today. You follow this up?"

"Of course; it was a lead. She had said to me if I wanted real answers then I should speak to this man. For all I knew, he was our guy—"

"Sure," Rosie said, interrupting him, "in a lot of cases the victims know their killer and is someone they trust. Could easily have been your guy."

"Exactly," he said, taking the card from her and tapping it against his leg, "so I went to see him, and he's one kooky bastard, I can tell you that much."

"So what did you get out of him?"

"Well, nothing, or so I thought at the time. He just raved on about demons taking one's soul by toying with and terrifying them. It just seemed like a guy with too much time on his hands and with too many people around him believing in his bullshit. I simply assumed he had already been in conversation with the mother and, well, y'know…"

"Projection," she said with a nod.

"Yeah, precisely; he was just projecting what she had told him, or it was what he had convinced her to believe. And I wasn't about to run the crazy old bastard in for selling powdered rhino horn to get your old man up in the night, as disgusting as the practice is, so I tagged his name in the database and flagged as a dead-end lead."

"Except, now…"

"Except, now I'm thinking we give Witch Doctor Kalisha a call and pay him a visit, especially off the back of something he said that has me freaked the fuck out."

Rosie stared at him, expecting him to follow up his statement. She shrugged. "Which is?"

Scott wet his lips and swallowed. "'When the grinning, white-faced demon comes-a-callin', you won't have long until he must be sent away.'"

Rosie stared at him, mouth agape and eyes wide, then blurted, "Fuuuuck me!"

"Yeah," Scott replied, nodding, "fuck me, indeed."

She turned away and looked down, as though the answers she was searching for resided in the bed sheets. "So, this is a demon then? This shit is real?" She gave a pained smile. "My God, that sounded so corny."

"Well… maybe a little." He smiled." But the fact remains, no matter how clichéd it sounds, what we are dealing with goes way beyond the understanding of the world as we know it. In truth, as terrifying as this all is, the other side of the coin has me scared out of my mind."

"What do you mean?"

"What do I mean?" He scoffed a little, not in relation to Rosie's question, but more the answer he was about to give her. "I mean, if demons are real, then all the other stuff has to be – and that means angels, and that means God. And that means… well, it means that I am panicking at some of my life choices and the things I have had to do in my past. My career didn't start in the F.B.I., Rosie; I had quite the military venture before that, one that took me to dark, dark places." He offered a worried half-smile, then looked down at his hands.

Abruptly, she reached over and grabbed his hands, forcing him to look into her eyes. "Look. Whatever you did in your past, I am sure it was for the best of reasons…" He rolled his eyes and drew in breath, responding with a crooked smile, but she was having none of it. "I don't care, Denver, really I don't. I may have only known you for a day but I'm pretty sure you're not marked for condemnation."

"How?" he said, his mouth cocked at one side. "Hmm… how do you know that, Rosie? How do you know that I haven't done some of the most terrible, terrible things, huh?"

She let go and sat back; her lips pressed tight together. She shrugged. "Okay. I don't. Fine, you're right. But what good is any of this going to do us, huh, this self-pity? And if you do have a lot of red in your ledger, then don't you think stopping whatever this fucking thing intends to do could clear it? Could wipe it clean?"

He stared at her for a few moments, then smiled and nodded. "Okay. Okay. Dr Kalisha lives in New York City. No point in heading out right now – might as well try to get some sleep. I'm sure if this demon wanted us out of the way he would have already done it, so it appears we have a grace period. And I for one intend to use the time it appears to have given us to find out how the fuck we stop him. Agreed?"

She nodded and smiled, though she suspected its lack of conviction betrayed her uncertainty.

Scott sat up straight and gave Rosie a smile of his own, though he did his best to convey more optimism within it. "Okay. Good enough. We'll head out before first light and give ourselves time to square this away. I have a feeling that him showing himself to me, has brought me into whatever he has in mind and I don't like being the one without the answers."

She nodded in agreement.

He paused. "Okay; I'll take the couch, and…"

Rosie held up a hand. "It's fine, Captain Chivalry – I'll grab the couch and you have your bed. I'm shorter than you and that couch looks uncomfortable. Since you'll be doing the driving, I'd feel better if you get the most amount of sleep possible."

Scott smiled, stifling any protestations he may have had. "Okay. You're the boss."

"Funny; and here's me thinking you were." She smirked.

"Hey, sister. About an hour ago I thought we were looking for a guy, now I'm about ready to hook us up with a priest and pray for absolution–"

"No priests," she retorted sharply. "Just… no priests."

He frowned for a moment, then remembered what the demon had told her. He offered an apologetic sigh and a nod, then walked into the bathroom.

She sat on the couch and took a deep breath, her fingers steepled under her nose. "Just… no fucking priests," she whispered.

16

Thursday 8ᵗʰ November 2012, 07.20am.

They had driven in silence for the most part, each wrestling with internal arguments related to the fantastical situation and trying to make sense of it in their own ways.

Rosie had been doing her best to not damage her calm following Scott's words the previous night, but they kept niggling at her, tapping at the back of her mind and not letting go, forcing their way to the front of the pack, demanding answers. She had to confront them. Had he been right? If there were demons, then there had to be angels, and that meant there had to be a God. That revelation had her searching her memories, trying to determine what level of terrible things she had done in her own past. Not only that – what constituted good and evil? Who got to decide? She had been involved in five shooting incidents in her time as a law enforcement officer, three of which had resulted in the suspects' deaths, and now she had begun second-guessing if she had been in the right. Sure, the courts and hearings had proven her blameless – she had followed protocol and procedure and had obeyed the rules of engagement to the letter – but maybe God wasn't so forgiving. Maybe God didn't take kindly to anybody taking a life, no matter the circumstances. Who was she to judge who should live or die? Who was she to determine what was right or wrong and end a person's existence? The laws of men were just that, and maybe God didn't see it the same way. More importantly, if He didn't see it that way, then his counterpart sure as hell would; and that was the problem – what acts did the Devil deem suitable for Hell?

She closed her eyes and shook her head.

Scott noticed. "Wrestling with the parameters of good and evil, are we?"

"Jesus, Denver, you should take that shit on the road." She glanced at him and half-smiled, then resumed staring out of the passenger window. "Is it that obvious?"

"Only because that's all I've been doing since last night, and I can spot a kindred spirit. Really makes you think, don't it?"

"Yeah. It really does." She continued to watch the world fly by. She pondered for a moment, then looked back at him. "I wonder who he meant."

"Who?" Scott asked, turning to her briefly before returning his attention to the road ahead.

"Last night, the demon said something like, 'once he has her, once he has the child' or whatever. I just wonder who he meant."

Scott frowned. "Well, the Devil, I assume."

She shook her head "No, not Him – that part I get... I meant *her*, I wonder who he meant by 'her'? 'Once he takes her.'" She sighed and stared out of the window again. "I hate not knowing shit."

Scott glanced at her again, nodding.

Nothing more was said for the twenty minutes it took them to reach and cross the Williamsburg Bridge and then enter the Tribeca area of New York City. Scott then navigated to an underground parking garage under the Woolworth Building on Barclay Street, close to Dr Kalisha's address, and pulled into a vacant space.

Getting out, Rosie was grateful for a big old stretch; her night's sleep on the motel couch had been less than stellar and had given her back and neck pain. She rolled her neck with a groan, trying to work out the kinks. Then she turned her attention to Scott. "He far from here?"

"Nah," he said, opening the rear, driver-side door and taking out his jacket and slipping it on. "Just a few blocks down."

She nodded, then followed him as he walked around the vehicle and set off toward the exit.

Upon leaving, they turned onto Barclay Street, and Rosie was happy to see that it wasn't jam-packed with people all pushing and shoving, like it would be in more dense-populated areas of the city. She was used to a slightly quieter life back in New Babylon, and the ferocity of some parts of New York City was something she had never gotten used to. She had been there many times before and, on each occasion, had been glad to leave. As incredible a city as it was, it was just too fast-paced for her, and she never really settled when visiting – but here in the Tribeca, although plentiful with people, it was okay for her and just enough to bear.

Rosie began hopping, and realized that something was in her shoe, perhaps a small stone or piece of grit. She grunted her displeasure, then hobbled to lean against the side of a building, lifting her foot to take off her shoe. Looking up, she realized Scott hadn't noticed her stopping. "Denver," she called, still wrestling with her shoe, "hang on a second."

He turned to see her propped up against the wall, then moved toward her just as she completed her task and pushed herself off the wall to set off toward him. In doing so, she bumped into what appeared to be a homeless man wearing a dirty combat jacket and jeans, and even dirtier shoes.

Rosie grunted, the man's burly frame punting her backward slightly. "Excuse me, pal," she said, somewhat angrily, "why don't you watch where you are going?"

The bearded, disheveled man stared at her for a moment, then narrowed his eyes and frowned. "You have a shadow about you," he said, looking her up and down. "I'd do something about that if I were you, and quick."

Rosie stared at him wide-eyed.

Scott pushed his way to her side. "Hey buddy," he said, moving the man back with a firm hand to his shoulder, "be on your way, or we'll have you run in."

The man looked him up and down and scoffed. "You, not so much. Just a little," he said. Then he turned and walked away.

"Goddammit, this city," Scott said as he watched the homeless guy walk away. "It's tragic 'n all, in many cases, but these guys are friggin' everywhere. You okay, Hendricks? He take anything?"

Scott's question jolted Rosie back to life; she had been staring after the man. She checked her jacket pockets. "No. No, he hasn't taken anything." She continued staring as the man walked further along the street, then turned toward her briefly before heading into an alleyway.

"You okay?" Scott said, moving in front of her and blocking her view.

She shook her head, then looked at him. "I can't explain it, but that man…" She looked past Scott, to where she had last seen the man.

"There was something about him. I just can't put my finger on it. But there was something extraordinarily strong about his presence – I guess you could say, his aura."

Scott smiled a little and seemed about to say something.

"No, fuck you, Denver. Don't do that, not after what we've seen. I'm serious – there was something about that guy that freaked me out."

There was no hint of mockery when Scott said, "Okay. Well, what did he say to you?"

"He said I had a shadow about me, and I should do something about it, and quick."

Scott's eyes widened. "Okay. Okay, bit weird and random." He looked toward the alleyway. "You wanna go after him and ask him some questions?"

She considered this for a moment, then conceded, "No. No, I don't. I don't think it would matter." She stared at the entrance to the alleyway for a few seconds as people moved around her, then she turned back to Scott. "Come on, let's just get to Kalisha. This fucking day is creeping me out enough without this shit."

Scott glanced at the alleyway one last time. "Yeah. Yeah, agreed. Come on."

They moved hastily through the bohemian, trendy Tribeca streets, Rosie's attention darting from one shop to another, sad that she wasn't able to stop and browse; she could have really done with some retail therapy. After about ten minutes they reached their destination: a steel door with a closed viewing port in it, in a relatively clean and well-kept back alley which was very much typical in one of New York's wealthiest zip codes.

Rosie looked the alley up and down as Scott rapped his fist on the door; the typical forceful manner of law enforcement. "Expensive area," she said with a nod and downturn of her mouth. "Doesn't really scream voodoo witch doctor territory."

Scott smirked and nodded, before returning his attention to the door and banging it hard once again. He was about to do it again when the viewing port slid open with a clack and the intense-looking eyes of a young black man stared back at them.

"Hey there," Scott said, taking out and flipping open his ID. "I'm Special Agent Denver of the F.B.I., and this is Detective Sergeant Rosie Hendricks of the West Babylon P.D. We wish to speak with Dr Kalisha."

The slat closed with a clack and Scott turned toward Rosie, who shrugged. He returned the gesture.

Their attention snapped back to the door at the sound of many locks disengaging. Then the door opened.

"Follow," a young Haitian man said and the owner of the face in the slat, and he walked off quickly down the narrow corridor.

"Nice place," Rosie said as she followed Scott through the door and saw that the plaster on the walls was broken and cracked. He turned and cocked his head to one side, as if asking for a little more decorum. She raised her eyebrows and pressed her lips together, the look suggesting a sarcastic 'sorry' and closed the door behind her.

As she passed through a curtain of wooden beads, she was pleasantly surprised at how clean, neat, and orderly the room into which she had been led was, and became a little annoyed at herself for being too judgmental. She took a deep sniff of the pleasant wooden and earthy incense aroma and raised her eyebrows again at Scott, though this time it was a gesture of gratification. She glanced around the room, admiring the many Haitian statues and pieces of art dotted about. Beautiful paintings hung on every wall and the room had an incredibly positive and relaxing feel about it, which seemed to melt all her troubles away.

The young man turned back to them and held up his hands, palms out at them, signaling for them to wait. Then he walked off briskly through another curtain of wooden beads that clacked together as he passed through them.

Rosie turned toward Scott. "It actually is a nice place," she said with a smile. "I was being a bit of a dick back there, I suppose."

Scott offered her a sympathetic smile. "Yeah, initial impressions can always be deceiving, huh?"

"Indeed they can be," an older male Haitian voice said. Its owner then drifted through the beaded curtain. "I have been expecting your return, Special Agent Denver. I assume it is Akoman who you wish to discuss?"

Scott looked at Rosie, his mouth open and his eyes wide.

17

Thursday 8th November 2012, 07.55am.

"Please… take a seat," Dr Kalisha said, gesturing to a round table with six chairs dotted around it. He watched as the officers accepted. He took the seat next to Rosie and turned to the young Haitian male, who had re-entered the room, speaking to him in Creole. The young man then scurried away through the curtain of beads.

"Some ginger tea will soothe our minds and set us on the right path," Dr Kalisha said.

"Oh, that's okay…" Rosie began, glancing at Scott.

"Nonsense!" Kalisha responded, waving a hand. "It is very good, very Haitian way of calming the soul, and I fear we will need much calming before the day is done."

Rosie smiled away her protestations as the young man returned carrying a tray containing a small teapot and three cups on saucers. He laid them onto the table gently and distributed the cups and then poured the tea.

"Mèsi, Emmanuel," Kalisha said, with a smile, "tanpri, kontinye ak kèk travay lap fè ou."

The young man nodded dutifully and disappeared back through the curtain.

Dr Kalisha turned back to his two visitors and smiled. "Ah, my apologies," he said with a wave of his hands, "Emmanuel does not speak much English. I simply asked him to carry on with his chores."

"What is that, Creole?" Rosie asked.

"Trè byen, Miss Hendricks. Very good. You know Creole?"

She shook her head. "No, no. Just… knew a guy… once. It doesn't matter." She smiled to move the conversation on.

"Ah, I see," Kalisha said. "Well, no matter. We will be undisturbed from here on." He leaned toward Rosie and gave a heavy sigh. "Now then, young miss," he said, taking her hands in his, "it seems the shadow has found its way to you."

Rosie sat up straight, her eyes wide. She was about to repeat what the homeless man had said to her on the street, but then Kalisha continued, "A dangerous demon is this one, very dangerous. Very dangerous indeed."

"Are there non-dangerous demons?" Scott said with a wry smile.

"Au contraire, Special Agent Denver—"

"Scott. Just… Scott will do, Dr Kalisha."

He responded with a hearty laugh. "Very well, Scott. In that case you must just call me Wilson and we can be done with all formalities, no?"

Scott smiled and nodded.

"But to answer your question, Scott – yes, there are very different types of demon, very different. Some of the lower level ones can only manipulate the world around them; be the flea in someone's ear and not directly influence them by action, whereas others, like our terrible friend Akoman, can do much worse. Much worse. And it seems that he has taken a shine to you, Miss Hendricks."

Rosie smiled and raised her eyebrows. "Rosie."

Wilson smiled and nodded. "Of course. No more dutiful pleasantries. Mwen eskizem."

Rosie sat forward a little, her hands still cupped in Wilson's. "Akoman – that's his name?"

Wilson nodded. "Yes. And he is a powerful demon, a powerful one indeed."

Rosie sighed and shook her head. "So, what does he want with me?"

Wilson let go of her hands and stood, then walked to a bookcase containing many volumes of varying shapes and sizes. Rosie turned toward Scott, who raised his eyebrows and shook his head

Wilson began leafing through a weighty tome. "Akoman is a dangerous and dark entity; he is a presence of pure evil intention whose purpose it is to corrupt the mind through fear, and turn his victims against themselves. His appearance among men has always signaled the coming of very dark times: plagues, wars, terrible dynasties – all of these have the taint of Akoman. If he is here among us, then things are very bad indeed."

Scott sighed. "Define 'very bad indeed', doctor. I mean, what are we looking at here?"

Wilson scoffed. "You need more to go on than the systematic eradication of the human population, Agent Denver?"

Scott looked down, as if he were a scolded child. "No... no, of course not, but..." His eyes darted as he tried to find the right words, but he could not. He had been used to being stumped on a case before, but this was brand-new territory. For one of the first times in his adult life, he felt lost and utterly helpless. The part of his mind that could crack a case wide open using logic, reason and pure investigative work told him this was too big, that the stakes were too high, and that he was in way over his head. But another part of him needed to know – had to, in fact. He looked back up at Wilson. "Please. Help us here. Help us understand what we are dealing with."

Wilson returned to his seat. "I intend to, Scott, please be assured of that. I intend to." He dropped the book onto the table with a thud. "Akoman is one of Satan's most trusted generals. An ashen-faced, smiling monstrosity who preys on the mind of his victims before murdering them mercilessly. You must understand, there are not volumes upon volumes written about this creature, for once his work is done, he is gone, leaving only an idea in the minds of men. But those who have put quill or pen to paper and noted his presence have all described him in the same way. The descriptions of the manner in which he kills his victims have not changed over the centuries. Here, look." He spun the book around then lifted it slightly and pointed to a page, drawing their attention to it. It depicted the exact way Scott and Rosie's victims had been murdered. Both stared at the image, mouths agape and eyes wide, then turned back to Wilson as he continued, "From here, what is noted, it appears there are eighteen victims to his cycle. But for all that is written, there is scant information about the process, other than how people are killed and that upon completion of the ritual, a great evil befalls the Earth, and man suffers the consequences, and it is Satan himself who determines the stakes and the horrors that will befall humankind. It was Zoroaster himself, an ancient Iranian spiritual leader and the only living soul believed to have bested the temptations of Akoman, who wrote that the aftermath of the demon's work directly correlates to the power that Satan possesses at that point in time." He looked into Rosie's and Scott's eyes in turn, lingering on each for a few seconds and studying their intent gazes, understanding that he had their fullest attention, "And I need not tell you two of all people that man's accumulated sins in this era are vast and many. I fear that Satan has amassed much great and terrible power and that something truly catastrophic is on its way."

Rosie looked down for a moment, then stood then began pacing the room, her hand on her brow. "This is too big – too much. Surely something like this is not for us to deal with – two police officers. If Heaven and Hell truly exist – and trust me, I am now a believer – then surely the big man upstairs has someone to take care of this, like, I dunno, an angel or something?"

Wilson contemplated the question with raised eyebrows, then sighed. "Perhaps, Rosie. Perhaps. But this does not alter the fact that Akoman targeted you, and I fear an integral part of the forthcoming events will be determined by you. God may have a plan for you. And maybe you are worthy, both worthy, of championing this cause for him. Of defeating Akoman."

Scott rubbed his forehead. He felt tired, the influx of information wearing him down. "But how did you know that this was the demon Akoman? How do you know so much about this, about him?"

"Because, Scott, I am now a part of his grand design too, whatever that may be. After the death of her daughter, Mrs Mubatu came to me."

Rosie sat back down; her attention fixed on Wilson. "What happened?"

"Well, she came to me and told me that her daughter had told her she was being stalked by a white-faced demon, and the entity had eventually killed her. She wanted me to find out who it was and demand her daughter's soul back from the creature. So I consoled her and told her I would accept her request. I looked into all she had told me, and great dread filled my heart as the details began to unfold. A divination ceremony was then performed with artifacts of great power and importance to her daughter, Esther. Within the ceremony I reached out to the spirits of our ancestors to ask for their aid in finding the soul of the poor girl and help us send it to where it belonged, as Mrs Mubatu believed that the demon had taken it to Hell." Wilson swallowed hard. "It was then that the demon came. Smiling. Laughing. He told me that he had no intention of releasing Esther, and that her soul was destined for greatness, that it would bring about something of the highest importance and that her mother should be proud as it was to aid in the birth of the new world."

Rosie shook her head, her mouth hanging open. Then she swallowed and wet her lips. "But why her? What connected her to the others?"

Wilson responded with a tired laugh. "Why? Why any of them? As an officer of the law, it is your job to justify and find meaning in the actions of others and to wrap such actions up in a neat package so as to understand their nature. But even then, there are those who have no meaning and no purpose other than to sow chaos and destruction. Maybe he chose them for good reason, or maybe he simply chose them because he could. Maybe there are forces at work here that have put us all on a path of interwoven destiny, and maybe there are not. But no matter; the only importance is that he killed them in the manner he did – and I believe," he looked up at Scott, "that we are now up to fifteen victims?"

Scott nodded.

Wilson contemplated him for a moment. "Then I can only assume we will be the last three."

"What! Why?" Scott said, sitting bolt upright, his eyes wide. "Why do you believe us to be the final three?"

"Because, Scott," Wilson said, snapping the book shut, then standing and replacing it in the bookcase, "he has shown himself to us and I do not believe that he would do so without purpose."

"You don't know that," he replied.

"No, you are quite right, Special Agent Denver. But call it a hunch. You know, like your Detective Columbo. 'Just one more thing, ma'am', that kind of stuff."

Wilson grinned, and Scott and Rosie could not help but respond in kind, no matter the seriousness of the situation.

"Please," Wilson continued as he approached the table, "drink your tea. It will make you feel better and will ease your mind now that you are considering a universe of questions."

Rosie pressed her lips into a flat smile and took a sip of her tea. It was much nicer than she had expected. She looked up at Wilson. "So what can we do? I really want this thing off me, and I absolutely do not want to end up like the others."

Wilson tapped a finger against his lips and stared into a corner of the room for a few seconds. "We must lure it to a place of power where we can control its movements. Some place that is grand, with holy energy that would weaken it. Then I would push it back into the abyss with a ritual to dispel witchcraft." He stared at Rosie for a few moments, as if wrestling with the idea within his mind, deciding if would indeed work.

She looked at Scott for a moment, then turned back to Wilson. "And if that doesn't work?"

Her words seemed to jolt him out of his musings. He raised his eyebrows. "Then I expect we all shall die, and whatever is to come, will come."

"Jesus," Scott said, turning away with his hand on his forehead. "No fucking pressure, then."

Rosie looked at him. "We have to try, Scott. *I* have to try. I can't have my soul damned for an eternity. I don't want to end up like that."

Her voice began to crack, and Scott knelt before her, placing his hands on her shoulders. "Hey, hey! No one's soul is getting damned. We're gonna figure this out." He looked up at Wilson. "Right, doc?"

"Of course, my child. I am sure we can do this. I will search for a place of power, and Emmanuel can assist me in researching and understanding how Zoroaster came to defeat the demon. I am certain we will triumph."

Scott looked up at Wilson. "Okay. Fine, but we ain't just gonna sit here and do nothing. We want to help and try to find something suitable too. What are we looking for?"

Wilson returned to tapping his finger against his lips.

Rosie blew air through her lips, puffing her cheeks. "Well, the damn thing keeps taking me back to that house where I first encountered it in West Babylon. Perhaps that would be a good place?" She said, her gaze shifting between the two men.

"No, my dear," Wilson interjected quickly. "I am afraid that would not do. I very much doubt any place it had used for its own ends would offer us a spiritually clean environment. No. It must be some place that has stood for holy purposes and the good of people – and that is strong in pure and powerful energy."

"Soooo, a church, then?" Scott asked.

"No, Scott, not just a church. It needs to be brimming with spiritual energy, where great things have happened, where people have done amazing things in the name of God and have not just put dollars into a collection plate or asked forgiveness for their sins. Some of those places are just buildings; cold, tired buildings for people to while away their sorrows. No – it must be a place of great personal sacrifice where the humblest of people have put others before anything else even themselves, in the name of good and purity."

"Oh, great," Scott replied, "I'll just dig out my copy of Tobin's Spirit Guide and hook us right up. Piece of cake."

Wilson narrowed his eyes at him, then pressed his lips together tight as he glanced at Rosie.

"Never mind," Scott said with a slight shake of his head. "It's a Ghostbusters referen— Y'know what? It doesn't matter."

Wilson stared at him for a few seconds and then shook his head. "Okay, well, you work on your Tobin's Guide and I will get to work here, and I will call you as soon as I have something."

"How long do you think it will take?" Rosie asked. She stood, and Scott did the same.

"Honestly, my child, I have no idea. A couple of days, perhaps?"

"Do I have that long?" she said.

Wilson looked at Scott and then back to her. He shrugged.

"Look," Scott said, "let's just get back to the New York field office, which isn't too far, thankfully. We'll get to work on a portfolio of places based on Dr Kalisha's brief and see what we can dig up. Between the three of us, I'm sure we can nail this down ASAP." He glanced at Wilson. "You still have my card, my number, right?"

"I do, Agent Denver, I do."

"Great. Then you call me the very second you have something, and I'll do the same and we will get right on it, no matter the hour. Yeah?"

"Agreed," Wilson said. He turned to Rosie and placed his hands on her shoulders. He smiled at her, then waved his hands across her head, flashing them in a pattern and rippling his fingers. Then he closed his eyes and muttered an incantation. He opened them again and smiled. "For what it's worth, of course."

Rosie smiled half-heartedly and nodded. "Thank you."

Wilson was about to do the same to Scott, but Scott shifted his head away with an awkward smile. He leant closer to Wilson. "But while you're at it, doc, try to figure out what the hell this thing wants, or what it's working on, as it may give us an edge that we very badly need. And you need to move like your own life is on the line here please, yeah?"

Wilson smiled. "As I said, Agent Denver; it very likely is. It very likely… is."

18

Thursday 8th November 2012, 10.55pm.

Scott was irritated and stressed, and when that happened to this degree, his eyes were first to display the signs, so he gave them a good rub to try to liven them up. He stretched, his hands raised high into the air as he leaned back in his office chair. He yawned and glanced to his left as Rosie approached holding two mugs, walking carefully to avoid spilling the steaming contents. He smiled as she took great care in setting his mug down on his desk and then took a seat opposite him, at a colleague's vacant position. He had shown her to it earlier that day, the agent who usually occupied it being out in the field. He watched as she blew into the mug then gingerly placed her lips to the rim and tested the coffee, wincing slightly and then blowing once more before trying again. He liked Rosie. He knew that not only was she a good cop, but a good person, and the way she had conducted herself in the last twenty-four hours – especially knowing what kind of entity stalked her, or more to the point, them – had seen his respect for her skyrocket. Many in their situation would have simply crumbled and been unable to process the diabolical information that had been presented – hell, he was surprised that even he was holding himself together as well as he was – but not Rosie. No, she had been fixated on the root cause of the problem and finding a solution to it, rather than being driven by a selfish need for self-preservation that would see her wither and shrink within herself, forgoing her responsibilities as an officer of the law. Especially since the level of horror Akoman had subjected her to thus far had been so intense. But whatever was happening, whatever they had stumbled onto and had leeched onto her, it was big, and Scott could feel it would have ramifications for many people, perhaps the whole world. They had a duty to get to the bottom of it all and prevent whatever was about to happen.

Looking up from her coffee, Rosie caught him staring, but upon studying his face realized he wasn't really staring at her, more through her.

"Penny for them," she said, then took another sip.

Scott started, thinking she must have thought he was ogling her rather than being lost in thought. "Sorry," he said, shaking his head, then reaching for his mug. "Miles away, just thinking about stuff."

She smiled teasingly. "I know, that's why I asked for a penny for your thoughts," she giggled. "So what you thinking about?"

He laughed away his dumb response and drank before continuing. "I dunno. Nothing. Everything."

She pondered this for a second, then sat forward. "You found anything?"

He sighed and looked at his computer, then shook his head. "Honestly, I don't even really know what we should be looking for. The brief that Kalisha gave us wasn't exactly brimming with intel."

She laughed and drank more coffee. "I'm not even sure he really knows."

He agreed.

She glanced around the field office, which now contained only a handful of agents, all of whom were fixated on their screens, some furiously tapping away at their keyboards. "This thing is so messed up," she said. "You told anybody else?"

He smirked. "And say what? I'm struggling to comprehend the gravity of the situation myself, let alone explain it to anybody else. And I really don't want an office and desk in the basement with a picture captioned *I want to believe* pinned up behind me."

Rosie laughed.

"Besides, what the hell do you say? Hey everyone, we're being stalked by an ancient Babylonian demon. Anyone wanna pull double shift and help us slay it?" He smirked again.

"Is it?" she asked, with a smile.

He frowned. "Is it what?"

"Babylonian."

He shrugged and gave a playful smile. "I dunno. Whatever, man."

"No, I'm just curious," she replied, enjoying the playful banter, "as I would have thought the world-famous F.B.I. would have had a department for ancient Babylonian demons. Maybe run by an Agent Starling – fly, fly, Clarice." She chuckled.

Scott looked back at his screen. "Yeah, yeah. Ha, ha, very fucking funny," he said.

Rosie's sarcastic smile lingered, before continuing. "Nah, you're right and I know it all too well. They wouldn't even bother psych-evaling your ass on that one. You'd have a memo that said, 'Why are you reading this when you should be clearing out your desk?'"

He laughed." You got that right, sister. You got that right." He tapped away at his keyboard.

"Look," Rosie said, placing her mug onto the desk and sitting forward attentively. "Let's go over the brief one more time, see if we can't shake some cobwebs out."

Scott slid to the side in his chair to see her better. "Okay, and agreed. And since I've done much of the talking on this today, you go."

She moved her chair to the side too. "Okay. Right, so whadda we know?" She counted points on her fingers. "We know it must be on holy ground, and it must be uninhabited so as to not allow innocent people to get caught up in whatever the hell we'll be doing. It must be brimming with holy energy – whatever the hell that entails – and any of his old grounds or associated areas won't cut it, as they are likely tainted, so it can't be anywhere we've already been."

Scott gave a contemplative nod.

"So. Maybe we start looking for places steeped in history, where amazing things have happened – and that those places might not necessarily be outright associated with religion."

"Such as?" he said, leaning forward.

"I dunno. Ummm." She stared into the distance, as though waiting for the answer to come walking into the room with a big neon sign on its head. It didn't, so she then blew air through her lips. "Okay. Errr… such as, for example, where people tended to or helped those stricken with the worst kind of disease and did so at great risk to their own lives. Or, I dunno, a place where someone gave up everything in defense of civil liberties, or something. You know, total and utter selfless acts that created holy energy by the love of those involved, and not because someone deemed God lived there."

Scott sat back, nodding, his mouth downturned as he swiveled in his chair.

Rosie stood and paced the floor next to his desk. "So, maybe there's one of these types of places in New York or West Babylon, and maybe it's run down, or derelict almost, but the memory of those great and good deeds lives on within its walls. And lemme tell you, after the last twenty-four hours, I am willing to believe in *anything* right now, and I don't need a poster on a basement office wall to tell me that."

Scott smiled at her quip. "Okay. Great. Those seem like pretty well thought out search criteria, Detective Hendricks."

She nodded at him cockily. "Yeah. Well thought out. Sure." She chuckled.

Scott nodded. "Alrighty then. Let's stop searching for places of holy power, or holy energy, or houses of the holy, 'cos to be honest, the results I've been getting have been dogshit, apart from listening to a few great Led Zep tracks." He smiled. "And let's refine them a little and see if we can't knock this one out of the park."

"Alright," she said, returning to her seat and dragging herself forward to the desk.

19

Friday 9ᵗʰ November 2012, 01:07am.

Rosie groaned with irritation. "Goddammit; I can't tell if any of these places would work. I honestly don't know what I'm looking for, and I keep second-guessing myself."

"Yeah, same," Scott said without looking up from his screen.

"And I'm sick of my search results leading to Amityville. Fuck that place."

Scott sniggered, his fingers still furiously tapping away at the keyboard.

"Or that old leper colony on North Brother Island," she continued, "but fuck that place too. I'd rather tackle him on the subway and accept collateral damage than a scary-as-shit kinda place like that."

This time, Scott blurted a laugh and stopped typing. "Agreed. I got that search result too, and that place gave me the willies just looking at the pictures. Not sure I would want to step inside it to face down an ancient demon."

She responded with a tired laugh and leaned back in her chair, hands clasped behind her head. "That's the key, though, isn't it? Where the hell is a good place to face down an ancient demon? I mean; the guy could be in this goddamn room right now, watching us, waiting to kill us, or at least know exactly what we intend to do."

She laughed, but then stopped abruptly. She suddenly felt afraid, vulnerable; the police work in which they had been engaged for the last few hours had offered distraction, but now she remembered what this was about and her fear washed over her like a wave. She sat forward, staring nervously around the room. The other agents in the office had left, leaving just her and Scott, and now the office took on a new atmosphere, dark and foreboding; cold. An eeriness seemed to infiltrate her surroundings and all at once Rosie felt something was off – *wrong* – and her eyes darted as though she might be just about to see something, or some*one*, at the periphery of her vision. Then, she actually did start to see things. But every time her gaze landed on the area where she thought she had seen something, whatever that thing was she thought had been there had gone.

But there it was again, and her gaze snapped towards where she was certain she had seen movement. She sat forward, her breathing becoming more erratic, and a knot forming in her chest. Her fear was manifesting itself literally, and it felt painful; it was as she imagined a heart-attack might feel. Her fist shot to her chest and she breathed in deep. The action hurt. She pressed her solar plexus harder, but the pain got worse.

She stood. "Scott," she said, through grunts, moving to the side to see him behind his monitor.

As if on cue, her pain stopped – so quickly, in fact, that she looked down to her chest in surprise before snapping her attention back to Scott. He sat motionless, his fingers resting on the keyboard but not typing, and he was staring at the screen. The grim look on his face made Rosie recoil in revulsion. Her brain immediately told her what his still, locked face reminded her of: the Joker, from the Batman comics. The pictures she had seen, where his expression was wild: mouth wide and ready to perform his signatory maniacal laugh, his eyes stretched open to their limits, revealing more sclera than normal in a human, bloodshot with veins spreading like deep-red lightning strikes.

She took a terrified step back, then looked around. Again, she felt as though something was there, at the edge of her vision – but if she could indeed catch a glimpse of it, would she want to? A sound behind her and to her left made her spin around, in time to see the strip lights flick off. Others in the same area followed suit, extinguishing one by one, and in the resultant darkness she thought she could make out a shape. She strained her eyes to make it out.

Her fear turned to abject terror as more lights went out, the trajectory of their extinguishing moving toward her. She felt she had to get away, that to be caught within the darkness would be a very bad thing indeed. She turned to run but then cried out in fright, her hands shooting to her mouth.

Scott stood directly in front of her, his expression unchanged but not looking at her; more past her and into the darkness beyond. She edged to one side, her hands still cupping her mouth, and a small whimper escaped her as Scott raised a hand and pointed at the darkness. His head then slowly turned toward her, though his eyes remained locked, causing them to turn pure white as they rolled to the side and into their sockets.

When he spoke, his voice was raspy and strained, although his mouth remained locked open in its terrifying grin. "Go and see, Rosie. Go and see what he has for you. It's fun in there. It's great in there. It's warm... down there."

Tears spilled from Rosie's eyes. She inched away from the horrific sight in front of her. Her mind went into overdrive, telling her that it wasn't real, that it was a vision and nothing more, and that at some point she would find her way out of the madness. But she could not get away. What made it worse was that, for some inexplicable reason, her attention was drawn to the place in which Scott was pointing. She tried to look away, but found she could not, as though an invisible force held her head in place, daring her to see what would come next.

Around the office, the rest of the lights went out and the room was plunged into darkness save for a tiny spot of light emanating from a computer monitor close to where a form seemed to be stood in the darkness. Slowly, she took her hands from her mouth, her breathing labored. She jumped as tables and chairs screeched to the side, carving a path toward the computer monitor that now flickered as multiple images raced across its screen.

Still looking at her with his creepy white eyes, and even creepier grin, Scott floated toward the monitor, his head lolling like a marionette's, and his body turned to the right though his head still faced her, his gaze never straying from her direction despite the impossible angle of his body. As he arrived at the computer, he turned to the left slightly, his arm pointing at the screen. His body had performed a full rotation, his neck twisted like a macabre helter-skelter.

This unnerving action brought Rosie's terror to new heights. She took another step backward, her hands returning to cup her mouth. She felt that if she voiced her fear then that would be the end of her, and she would crumble to the floor. Despite her current situation, she still desperately wanted to retain even a modicum of control; she wasn't ready to give up just yet.

"Come see," Scott said, his grin growing even wider, accompanied by a sound like a balloon stretching. "Come see what he has for you."

Rosie gasped as her feet moved without her control. She knew she hadn't done it – she didn't want to get anywhere near him, or the screen – but all the same, her feet moved, and she found herself walking toward the monitor. She tried to fight against it, but could not; it was as though someone had grabbed each of her legs and was puppeteering them in turn.

"No," she cried out and grunted, wrestling against being controlled, but it was no good; struggling was pointless.

Scott turned briefly to look at the monitor as a raspy, whispered sound was emitted from it, then turned toward her. Somehow his eyes and grin had become even wider. He let rip a horrifying cackle, though his mouth did not move, and his eyes opened wider still to focus on her. Behind him, a dark shape moved forward and then stepped into the feeble light.

Akoman's chalky white face held a terrifying grin, and his blood-red tongue danced over his razor-sharp teeth. His hand appeared above Scott's head and his fingers wriggled, mimicking the actions of a puppeteer, and Scott reacted accordingly, performing a macabre jig while continuing to grin at Rosie. Then Akoman performed a snipping action under his hand, as though his fingers were scissors, signaling his abandonment of his puppet. Scott collapsed to the floor, his gaze still fixed on Rosie even as he lay crumpled in a heap.

She cried out again as her legs moved faster, as though they were eager to get her to the monitor and see what it had to offer, despite every fiber of her body screaming otherwise. When she reached the screen, she stopped, and Akoman leaned forward to her. She could smell his breath – foul, noxious, sickening – and she retched.

"Who do you trust?" he said, his voice deep and slow. "Him?" He glanced down at Scott. "The witch doctor? Who?" He moved behind her and placed his hands onto her shoulders, each finger resting in place one by one.

Rosie flinched at his touch. His hands felt hot – *extremely* hot. She tried to shrug him off, but could not, and a whimper escaped her lips.

"You try to fight me, but still you do not understand your purpose, or even the game. You do not know what it is you must do, or, in fact, what it is you have been chosen for. Your calling is great, Rosie; you should be proud."

Finally, she shook off her fear enough to find her voice, though she spoke through panting breaths. "Proud? I should be proud? Of what? There is no version of this story in which you are anything other than an evil fuck trying to kill me, so why don't you spare me your bullshit and tell me what it is you are actually doing?"

Although she was filled with terror, the cop part of her mind was doing its best to rear its head and take control of the situation. That rational portion told her that this thing wasn't going to kill her – not right now, at least – as it needed her. With that knowledge, she should try to glean as much information from it as possible. That was the confident cop side of her. However, the scared, non-cop part faltered and she breathed erratically again.

Akoman chuckled. "See. Even when you are trying to be brave, you cannot be. You are a charade, a walking contradiction well aware of your inner faults; flaws that you have made available to me. You cannot accomplish anything, and you cannot do more than I command. You are mine to use as I will, young Miss Hendricks. So I ask you again, who can you trust? Them, your so-called friends, your allies? Or me, the one who controls you and has your best interests at heart?" He laughed again.

Rosie grunted, though couldn't disguise her anxiety as she replied, "My best interests at heart? Are you fucking kidding me? You don't own me and you sure as hell don't know me. This is fucking puppetry, and you have no power over me. *I* control me." She took a step backward and almost laughed aloud with nervous delight as she felt her legs returning to her control.

"My, my, child, you are a feisty creature. Look at you, fightin' back." He roared with laughter.

"Fuck you, you powerless bastard!" she blurted, and took another step back.

Akoman's face darted forward to hers, his features transforming into his hideous demonic state, his teeth larger than ever and poised to clamp onto her head. "DO NOT FUCKING TEST ME, CHILD, OR I WILL DEVOUR YOU RIGHT HERE, RIGHT NOW."

Her eyes snapped shut and she leaned away from his fury, crying out.

Akoman's head moved back, and his face returned to its neutral, yet still unnerving, state. Rosie's eyes inched open though she still reeled from him.

"No. No," he said. "The delight of death is not for you… yet. And besides," he motioned toward the screen, "Daddy wants a word." He slinked backward into the darkness and then he was gone.

Rosie let out a tearful sigh and raised a trembling hand to her lips. Then she looked at the screen. On it she saw a room with no carpet, just wooden boards, with a bed in the middle and meagre furniture dotted around. She moved closer to the monitor, wondering what it was she was meant to be seeing. She looked away from the screen and around the office, unsure whether Akoman really was gone or if, in fact, he was lulling her into a false sense of security, waiting to strike. Satisfied that he wasn't skulking in the darkness, she turned her attention back to the monitor. This time, however, a man sat on the bed. It was her father, with a young-looking girl sitting facing him, their gazes locked on one another. As though sensing that Rosie was now watching, he turned his attention slowly toward her, then smiled before he turned back to the child and leaned in to kiss her.

Rosie began to sob, repeating the word "No," over and over. She tried to look away as the kiss became more passionate, but she just couldn't, nor could she seem to close her eyes; she was forced to watch the most vile and revulsive act imaginable as her father ran a hand over the girl's body, groping her breasts and then slipping it between her legs. As tears rolled down Rosie's cheeks, her father turned toward her once more, his mouth still locked on the young girl's, and he smiled at her. He then moved away from the girl a little and spoke to Rosie.

"Hey, peanut. I wanted it to be you, but I guess she just had to do."

Rosie felt sick, violently so, and her stomach felt like it would explode. Her throat convulsed and she dry heaved through her sobs.

"But now you can join us," her father continued. "Now you can come and play with us."

Then he grabbed hold of each of the girl's cheeks and pulled, peeling the skin off her entire face in one go. The young girl did not scream, or even react; she just allowed it to happen as though oblivious to the entire thing. Slowly, Rosie's father raised his hand to admire the young girl's detached face, and then he looked back to Rosie and smiled. His free hand reached toward the screen, slowly at first, his fingers wiggling in the air, but then as it neared the surface of the screen, it shot out and clamped onto her arm.

Rosie shrieked in terror as pain blistered up her arm and into her mind. She felt extreme heat. Her attention snapped to the screen, where her father roared with laughter. He was still sitting on the bed, which was now on fire, along with the rest of the room. The young girl screamed and writhed on the floor as she burned to death.

"Come join us, you fucking bitch!" her father screamed as he yanked Rosie toward the monitor.

Rosie screamed once again and slammed a hand against the desk, fighting against her father's pull with everything she had. But she was losing, and could feel herself moving toward him. Her face contorted into a grimace of determination and her eyes closed as she fought against his powerful pull, the horrifying pain of fire burning up her arm all the while. She opened her eyes to see that the screen was just beyond the tip of her nose, her father's blurred face pressed against it on the other side.

"Fucking get in here, you little cunt!" he shouted, and Rosie screamed.

****

She flailed her arms, screaming, as Scott shook her shoulders and shouted into her face, "Rosie. Hendricks. Wake up. Wake the fuck up."

She ceased her erratic movements and stared at him, eyes wide and holding her breath. Finally, she exhaled and began to sob. "Oh my God, Scott. Oh my God, it was so real. It was so goddamn real." She threw her arms around him and embraced him, burying her head into his chest, still crying.

They remained that way for a few moments while she gathered herself. Then, finally, she peeled away from him and wiped her eyes.

"It felt so real," she said again. "That was so terrifying. It felt so real." She looked down and fiddled with her hands.

Scott swallowed hard, then wheeled over a chair and sat. "Maybe that's because it was," he said.

She looked up at him, brow furrowed, her mouth slightly open.

He took a deep breath, then leaned forward. "My phone rang. It was Kalisha, so I answered it quickly. He had told me he found what we are looking for. So I stood up and turned away from you just for a moment, then turned back to get pen and paper to write the location down and you had gone – vanished."

"What?" she said.

"Yeah. Gone. I wrote the place down quickly and told Kalisha I had to go and would ring him back. Then I just started shouting and looking for you. You were nowhere to be found. I searched this floor high and low, but you had gone. I didn't know what the hell to do, so I raced back here thinking I would call Kalisha and ask what the fuck was going on, how you could just vanish and could he help me. And there you were, screaming in your chair and trying to push your fucking hand into the monitor screen. Rosie, you freaked me the fuck out and I don't mind admitting it. Not least because your goddamn arm was smoking. Look!" He pointed to a spot on her arm.

Rosie winced as she saw the finger marks burned into her flesh. Immediately, she went to touch it, but then hesitated, not wanting to feel the pain. She ran her fingers gently over the mark and looked up at Scott in surprise. "It doesn't hurt. What the fuck, Denver? It doesn't hurt. But that's where his burning hand grabbed me. But it doesn't hurt."

"Who?" Scott asked. "Whose burned hand?"

"My father's." She looked away. "Akoman was here, and you were…" she glanced at him, "…different."

Scott stared at her for a few moments, then swallowed hard and reached over to his desk, grabbing a Post-it pad. He waved it at her, showing the message. "This is where Kalisha wants us to meet. A place in upstate New York called Cazenovia."

"Upstate? Why so far?"

He shook his head. "I dunno. I was too busy looking for you to ask. But this is where he said we needed to be. An old manor house in Cazenovia. Said he would meet us there in the morning, as he had to go prepare and get some specific things."

Rosie turned away, pondering. "Can I trust you, Denver?"

"What?" Scott retorted.

"Exactly as I asked. Can I trust you?"

"Can you trust me? What the fuck does that mean? Of course you can trust me."

She stared at him.

"Rosie, what the fuck? What the hell did that thing say to you?"

She continued staring at him, then caved, her body wilting. "I don't know. I'm sorry. I'm just exhausted and I don't know what's what anymore. Whether up is down or left is right." She placed her hands over her eyes. "I feel like I'm losing my fucking mind, Denver. Like I am losing… my… fucking… mind!"

Slowly, he bent on one knee and placed his arms around her shoulders to embrace her. "You can trust me, Rosie. I got your back and we will beat this thing, together." He moved her away and gently removed her hands from her eyes. "Look. It's a little over a four-hour drive to Cazenovia. Let's try to get some shut-eye, if possible, rest up and then head up there around five a.m. I'll drive. And let's finish this thing. For both our sakes."

She offered a strained smile, nodded, then took a deep breath and gently eased him away from her so she could stand. She stretched her lower back out and glanced around the office.

Scott smiled. "There's a couple of half-decent couches in the canteen area. Come on. I'll show you."

She nodded again and followed him.

****

Akoman hovered and grinned outside one of the windows.

"It's almost time," he said before floating away, his posture mimicking Christ on the cross.

20

Friday 9th November 2012, 08:34am.
Rosie laughed at yet another of Scott's jokes. The drive had proved more of a fun distraction than she could have possibly hoped. In the hours they had spent travelling to Cazenovia, he had surprised her with his adeptness at comedy – not so much joke-telling, more back-and-forth banter displaying his razor-sharp, dry wit. The latest bout had amused her the most. She turned to look out of the window, her foot raised against the dashboard, and smiled, grateful to put the horrific events she had experienced in the F.B.I. office behind her. She had been silently praying that there would be no repeat of that terrible incident and that she wouldn't see any further visions of her dead father in the most horrible of circumstances, but her rational side knew that it would not be the case. The demon, Akoman, had her number now, and it would play on that aspect of her fear and insecurity for all his worth to achieve his endgame. She knew she had to be stronger when they next met. She needed to be thicker-skinned and more adept at circumventing fear; if Scott was right, then that was the major element in the battle against the demon. *Deny it oxygen through fear, cut off its food supply* – as he had put it – *and starve the damn thing to death*. It was only a theory, and maybe Wilson could shed more light on it when they finally hooked up with him in Cazenovia – but it was all they had right now, and Rosie felt much more comfortable having a plan, whether or not it proved useless. All cops preferred order to chaos.

She gazed out of the window. Not all of the beautiful foliage had yet been gripped by winter. She still saw plenty of green from pines, interspersed with Norway Spruce, the trees almost forming a canopy around them, such was the density of the forestation on this leg of the journey between Sherburne and Otselic in New York State. She pondered the magnificence for a moment before turning to Scott.

"I guess He did do a good job after all," she said, smiling.

"Who?" Scott responded, glancing at her quickly.

"Well, God, of course," she said, looking back out of the passenger side window.

"Or She," he replied, smiling. "Could easily be a She. At least that's what Alanis Morrisette would have us believe." He smirked.

Rosie smiled and leaned her head back a little, staring at him for a few moments. "Ahhh, a Kevin Smith fan, I see."

"What? Are you kidding me! *Dogma* is the best, man, the absolute best. *Clerks* was good, but *Dogma* rules. Snoogins." He said, then smiled.

Rosie laughed. "I wouldn't have pegged you for a Smithy."

He smiled. "Why not?"

"Aww, I dunno, because you're F.B.I., I guess." She held her arms out in front of her, "We here at the F.B.I. have no sense of humor of that we are aware of," she said in a faux-robotic voice.

Scott chuckled. "Ohhh, fuck you, Hendricks. We're funny guys. Damn funny guys, as you have attested on this journey, by nearly peeing in your knickers."

She nodded and laughed.

"It's just those damn crime programs on TV – they always seem to pick the stiffs to represent us." He laughed again.

Rosie returned to looking out of the window, still smiling. "But… it makes you wonder, though, yeah? The whole Heaven and Hell thing."

He took a deep breath. "Yeah. It does. Like I said at the motel, I got red in my ledger."

She pondered him for a moment, empathy and slight sorrow for him rising up inside her. Thoughts of his past must be eating away at him. She wondered whether she should even try to broach it. She was going to dismiss it for fear of upsetting him, but then thought *What the hell – under the circumstances, what harm could it do?* and jumped in with both feet. "What is it about your past, Denver, that has you so spooked?"

He huffed a small laugh and clucked his tongue a few times. "Yeah. That," he said, then gave another small laugh. "Nail on the head there, Hendricks. Nail on *the* head: A spook. I was one, back in the day. Real, deep black-ops shit, and I was asked to do some fucking awful things for my country."

A shadow seemed to fall over his face, as though the very mention of his past had encouraged the old him to surface and take control, overwhelming the cool, calculated and funny agent she knew and replacing it with a terrifying killing machine. She knew enough about former military operatives who moved into law enforcement to know that what he described was an extremely dangerous person. She swallowed, hard. "Afghanistan?"

He glanced back at her, seeming somewhat surprised, then shook his head. "Tip of the iceberg. Tip... of the iceberg. That's where our government is happy to let the American people know we are operating. Truth is, we are *everywhere* and have our dirty little military mitts into everything."

"Like what?" she said, intrigue taking over, making her dare probe further. He sighed, and she assumed she had pushed too far. "Look, I'm sorry, Scott. You don't have to answer if you don't want to."

He cut her off. "No, no it's fine, 'cos somehow I get the feeling that none of that shit matters anymore." He took another deep breath. "Look. You're an intelligent cop – a *very* intelligent cop – so let me just say this, and then your intelligence can fill in the gaps: drugs and murder, amongst other things. People needed removing, and shit needed paying for. Okay? The war on terror doesn't come cheap."

She pressed her lips together and nodded. "Good enough." She resumed staring out of the window. She would never, ever ask him about it again.

Silence reigned for what seemed like hours but was, in truth, just a few minutes.

Eventually, Scott said, "You believe in God?"

She scoffed. "Well it's kinda hard not to, now, isn't it?" She laughed.

He shook his head. "No. I mean, do you believe in Him. We know He exists, or at least we can now surmise he does, but do you *believe* in Him?"

She pondered the question. It was a good one, a damn good one. Did she believe in God? Or better yet, could she now *allow* herself to believe in Him? Her strict religious upbringing had instructed her to, but when she had passed into adulthood and been allowed thoughts of her own, she had shunned the concepts of religion and God, outright refusing to believe. Her parents had been partly to blame, but her atheism could not be laid solely at their feet. No; that had been the fault of all humankind, or at least the most despicable examples of it. Every call she had attended in which some animal had murdered their child, gangland slaying after slaying, sometimes with innocent bystanders caught up in the horror… those had been the blocks of information that had eroded her belief in any notion of the Almighty. She knew, positively *knew*, that it was the actions of humans that were responsible and not some evil presence working against the other side; the divine. And so, she had locked religion into a box in her mind; wrapped it in chains and sunk it to the bottom of an ocean within her. But now… Well, now, everything had changed, the chains had broken, and that box had resurfaced and was bobbing around, begging her to reopen it and re-examine her faith. Would allowing it back into her heart help save her from what she was about to face? Would it help save them all? She could not be certain, but the one thing she knew to be true was that she could no longer deny it. Furthermore, in truth, this was what caused the greatest amount of pain: that her parents had been right all along and that her shunning of their beliefs and faith was absolutely wrong. She hated the fact that she could never apologize to them for that. Especially her mother. Particularly, her mother.

She looked back at Scott. "As a kid I used to believe in Him, used to think He was there, watching over me, comforting me, helping me make the right choices. But as time went on, and I distanced myself from my parents, so in turn I distanced myself from Him." She half-smiled. "I didn't believe in Him. But I do now. And I pray for His help, strength and guidance in the coming hours." She looked at Scott. "And you?"

He stared ahead, then offered the faintest of smiles. "I want to believe," he said.

Rosie laughed.

21

Friday 9th November 2012, 09:20am.

They both admired the colonial features of Cazenovia as they drove through the town center. Many buildings had been updated and modernized over the years, but the rustic undertones were still visible for all to see, providing quaint charm to their surroundings. Winter had found its way to the town to a much greater degree than other parts of their route, such as Norwich or Georgetown. Snow piles at the side of the road gave the game away, along with the cold-weather clothing of the handful of townsfolk who went about their business at a languid pace.

"Ooooh, I could see myself living in a place like this," Rosie said, taken aback. "Quiet, peaceful, probably little crime. Yup, this would be heaven."

Scott smiled. "On the surface. But they probably put outsiders in a wire mask and fill it with bees at harvest time."

Rosie laughed. "Don't be an ass, Denver. These folks will be good old-fashioned American people. Salt of the earth and friendly as hell. Mark my words."

He smiled, then glanced at the sat nav. "Place we're looking for is showing a little over three miles away. Other side of Cazenovia Lake."

Rosie gave a pained look. "Ugh, really need the bathroom. Can we stop first?"

He nodded. "Sure, sure. Need to go myself." He pointed ahead. "Look, as if by magic. A diner."

He pulled up outside the establishment and they got out and stretched, studying their surroundings, before walking inside. As they entered, a couple of people glanced their way, taking in the strangers that had just arrived, but their stares seemed more curious than antagonistic, unlike depictions of rural America in Hollywood movies. Rosie offered Scott an I-told-you-so look, to which he smirked and rolled his eyes. As if to further cement Rosie's earlier statement of how super-friendly the Cazenovia townsfolk would be, a pretty young blonde waitress greeted them with a smile from behind the counter.

"Mornin' folks. I'm Carol." She tapped her name badge to reinforce her statement. "Welcome to Billy's. What can I getcha?"

"Umm, hey there," Scott replied, looking slightly embarrassed, as he knew how his next words would come across. "Ahhh, we kinda only need to use your restroom." He pursed his lips apologetically.

"Hey, course, no problem. Bathroom's in the back." Carol pointed.

Rosie made a huge show of emphasizing her position on the issue of friendliness by smiling and widening her eyes unnaturally at Scott before heading off to the bathroom.

Carol's extra-courteous nature had the desired effect. Scott wondered if it had been her ploy all along, at whether the woman was a maniacal genius in the getting-customers-to-order-regardless department. He tapped the counter. "You know what, Carol? Why don't we also have a couple of cups of coffee to go, along with that bathroom break?"

Carol smiled, showing her perfect, gleaming white teeth. She really was a beautiful young woman in every sense. "Sure," she said, "you go do what ya gotta do, and I'll have the coffee ready."

Scott smiled and nodded, then ambled to the men's restroom.

Upon her return, Rosie saw Scott sitting at the counter with a cup of coffee in hand and another on the counter before an empty stool.

"Wow! You were fast, Denver," she said, grinning.

"Agh, dude's perks. Never takes us as long as you gals." He smiled back.

"We stayin' a while?" she asked as she took the seat next to his.

"What can I say," he said, Carol's quaint charm won me over."

Rosie smirked. "Fair enough," she said, and took a drink from her cup.

"So, you folks in town visiting?" Carol asked, her bubbly smile never wavering. "Or…"

Scott hurried to swallow his sip of coffee to answer her. "Ah, sadly nothing as fun as that. Business, unfortunately."

"You cops?" she asked, with a slight smirk.

Rosie chuckled. "That obvious, huh?"

"Agh," Carol said with a wiggle of her head, "you kind of have the presence of purpose about you. Most folks round here live a slower life, and the tourists that come… well… they look touristy." She laughed. "So yeah. You look like cops."

Scott nodded, smiling. "We're headed to Braithwaite Manor. You know it?"

Carol's bubbly demeanor lessened slightly, and her brow furrowed as her attention darted between them. "Why?" she said. It didn't seem a question, more meaning, *Why would you do a thing like that?*

Scott glanced at Rosie briefly before turning his attention to Carol. He smiled. "As I said. Business. The cop kind. It's on the other side of the lake, yeah?"

Carol continued staring at him, her mouth slightly open. "Yeah. Yeah. Other side of Cazenovia Lake." She took a breath, her smile returned. "Sorry, I must look weird, but no one goes there if they can help it. That place is creepy, and strange shit happens there."

"Yeah? What kind of strange shit?" Rosie asked, taking a sip of her coffee.

"Oh, y'know."

Rosie raised her eyebrows and shook her head a little. "No, not really. In fact, we were kinda expecting the opposite… a benign place."

Carol's eyebrows knitted together. "A whaaa?"

Rosie smiled. "Never mind, honey. But," she took another sip of her coffee, "we can't help it; we have to go. But thanks for the advice."

Carol's smile waned, then she pursed her lips and nodded. "Fair enough. Hey, just holler if you need anything." She walked to the other end of the counter on the understanding that their conversation was over.

Rosie smirked. "Well, that was very *Children of the Corn*-esque."

Scott nodded slightly. "Yeah. Bit weird, don't ya think?"

Rosie continued to study Carol, who had now turned her charms onto a couple of older gents at the end of the counter, who were laughing along with her. She nodded. "Yeah, it was. Not really what I would be expecting from somewhere Kalisha wanted for a holy place, if I am being honest."

"Agh," Scott said, "even a church is creepy as hell in the dark, when you're alone."

"Yeah, but she genuinely gave off a, *we-don't-talk-about-that-place* kinda vibe."

"Well. Let's go find out," Scott said. He polished off his coffee and stood abruptly.

22

Friday 9ᵗʰ November 2012, 09:44am.

"I can see why Carol the waitress was so freaked out," Scott said as he steered the car along the narrow track on the approach to the main gates of Braithwaite Manor. "Even the run up to the place is like a fucking horror movie."

"Creepy is as creepy does," Rosie whispered with a smirk.

"Very funny," he replied with a sideways glance.

"Just joking, buddy," she replied.

They continued along the uneven road bordered by dense lines of many tall pines from which an eerie mist drifted across the road in places. And as they drove through malevolent atmosphere, Rosie shuddered.

"Something doesn't feel right about this, Scott."

"I will *not* disagree with you there." He was about to say something else when the mist cleared to reveal two huge iron gates and, standing in front of them and resting against his car, was Wilson Kalisha.

"Well… this isn't the House on Haunted Hill at all, is it?" Rosie said, glancing at Scott.

"Jesus," Scott said, as he studied the foreboding, dilapidated baronial manor house.

Wilson waved to them as Scott eased his car to a stop next to the doctor's. He turned toward Rosie. "Okay, guess we get this show on the road."

She nodded and got out of the car, making her way toward Wilson. She took a moment to study the huge, rusted, arched iron gates, complete with a family crest wrought into the center of each one. A huge chain with a large, equally rusted lock secured them in place. She thumbed toward them while looking at Wilson. "Take it you got the keys, then?"

Her question clearly took him aback; his head tilted and he frowned. "What do you mean, Detective Hendricks? Why would I have the keys?"

Scott took a step toward him. "Because you got us here; so why the hell wouldn't you?"

"Me?" he responded, prodding a finger at his own chest. "It was you who called I, Agent Denver, and told me to meet you here and at this time."

Scott waved his hands in dismay. "Oh no, no, no, no, no. You called me last night and I had to hang up on you when Rosie had…" He trailed off, then snapped his attention to Rosie.

Almost in unison, they both said, "Trap."

"Ahhh, fuck's sake," Rosie proclaimed. She spun in circles, checking for the attack that was surely imminent. "Fucking, fuck's sake. Son of a bitch has brought us where he wants us to be. GODDAMMIT!" she screamed into the misty air. "Under no circumstances are we to go into that fucking house."

"Okay, okay," Scott said. "New plan. Let's get back to town, back to the diner, and figure this out there."

"I don't think that will be possible, Agent Denver," Wilson said, his voice a dry monotone.

"Why?" Scott said, reeling around to look at him.

"Because whatever is to happen, it will be in the house behind us." Wilson pointed back along the track in the direction from which they had driven.

Walking toward them, his arms stretched wide and a thick blanket of fog trailing him, strode a grinning Akoman, his eyes pure white and his signatory, unnaturally wide grin spread across his face. His grin then turned into a wide smile, and from his mouth came a loud, vicious scream that seemed to carry a legion of voices within it. His arms stretched even further, more than should have been possible, covering the distance to each tree line, making it clear there was no way past. To make matters worse, from out of the fog behind him padded multiple demons, jackal-like in nature but much, much bigger than any canine. From their open mouths dripped saliva, from between rows and rows of terrifyingly crooked and jagged teeth. They joined in with their master's screams of terror, adding to the horrifying cacophony.

Then Akoman stopped in his tracks, and with it the screeching ceased; the jackal demons now stood motionless beneath their master, their hulking frames heaving with deep breaths, as though they were eagerly anticipating the thrill of the hunt to come.

"I think we need to get inside now," Scott said as he backed slowly toward the gate.

"Agreed," Rosie replied. She turned and grabbed the chain and lock and gave it a massive shake. "It won't fucking budge!" she screamed as she rattled the chain.

"Maybe we can ram it with the car?" Scott said, moving back to the vehicle.

Akoman began to laugh; the sound was deep, demonic, and booming and echoed throughout the entire area, making Rosie, Scott, and Wilson put their hands over their ears, such was its crushing intensity. "Run, run, little piggies. I need you to run, run, run," he said, his smile wider than ever.

They spun around as the chain broke behind them, clattering to the ground. The gates creaked open. Then the laughter stopped, and they turned back toward Akoman while inching backward.

Akoman screamed. With that, the jackal demons charged, adding terrifying roars to their master's shriek.

"RUUUUUN!" Scott screamed. He took off through the gates at high speed, followed by Rosie and Wilson.

The fog thickened and intensified around them, rolling over them to form an impenetrable blanket that made each of the group to lose sight of the others, distorting all shapes within the fog.

"Scott?" Rosie screamed as he slipped out of view.

She heard him call her name, but not in response to her shout, more as though he was searching for her and hadn't heard her call. He sounded far away, despite him having been at her side only moments before. Then she heard Wilson call out both of their names, but once again she was unable to pinpoint his location. She turned in circles, listening intently for any sounds of the demons, aware that she had gotten turned around and had no idea in which direction the entrance to the manor was. Panic began to set in and her heart raced. She resisted the urge to cry, although she was right on the precipice of doing so, despair snapping at her, her mind telling her she wasn't strong enough to resist it and that she must succumb. She froze and closed her eyes, small tears beading, as a low growl sounded behind her. Gingerly, she turned around and took in a sharp breath: one of the jackal demons stood before her, grinning.

Her feet scraped backward, fear making her legs as heavy as boulders, and she inched away from the beast. She mouthed a silent prayer that it would not immediately attack, that it would behave like a dog, taking a moment to weigh up the power dynamic and assess the threat.

"Okay," she said, her voice broken and wavering, her hand moving slowly toward her holster for her weapon. "There's a good boy. Nice and easy, no need to get angry."

The demon grinned and began to chuckle.

Rosie ceased reaching for her gun. Her eyes widened as the creature spoke.

"Quick, quick, little piggy. Run."

At that moment she knew that drawing her weapon was not a good idea; she had to run. She turned and bolted from the creature, sprinting faster than she ever had before in her life; at such a pace that her lungs soon screamed for oxygen, but her adrenaline-fueled terror told them to get in line and continued to propel her forward at a blistering pace. From behind, she heard the creature give chase, hunting her and making her panic skyrocket. She vocalized that fear with high-pitched grunts and wails. Then, and much to her relief, she burst through the bank of fog to see Scott and Wilson linked together, crashing their shoulders into and then falling through the door to the manor. With renewed determination, she pumped her arms and legs even harder, racing toward the door and screaming, convinced that the demon was almost upon her and breathing down her neck. With one final scream, she launched herself into the air and dove through the open front door before it slammed shut behind her.

She scrambled away from the entrance on all fours, expecting the creature to burst through and tear into her. She was struggling to find enough energy to haul herself to her feet and tear off again; her lungs were on fire and her breathing was racing out of control.

But the creature didn't come. So, she just sat there, shoulders heaving from the exertion of trying to control her breathing, staring at the large, sturdy oak door. Her mind reeled at the realization at how dumb diving through the door could have been, had Scott and Wilson not been there to slam it shut behind her.

Then she realized that they were nowhere to be seen. The door must have shut on its own: the lobby was empty. She scanned her surroundings, then called out their names, hoping that they would come running from one of the doors to either side. But no answer came and nobody appeared.

Gingerly, she got to her feet and looked around again. She was in a large lobby of a grand building. The place was in a very poor state of repair, with rubble dotted all around and dirt and leaves blanketing the ground. Behind her rose a long, sweeping staircase leading to the first floor, with more branching stairways leading up at either side to the floors above. To the sides of the lobby were multiple doors that led off to God only knew where. She didn't want to put blind trust into opening them to find out.

"Scott! Kalisha!" she called again. But, as before, there was no answer.

Rosie started and cried out in fright as the front door took a gigantic pounding under the weight of something outside. Quickly, she drew her gun while slowly backing away, her gaze fixed firmly on the door. There was another huge shunt, followed by what she thought were voices speaking hurriedly outside. She swore they sounded like Scott and Wilson.

"Hello?" she called out, lowering her weapon slightly. "HELLO!"

There was no response, but she continued to back away little by little. Then, she inhaled sharply and held her breath, heat rising up the back of her neck and her eyes watering with fear as she backed into something large. Immediately, she recognized the foul odor of Akoman. Her eyes closed and tears rolled down her cheeks.

"Rosie. Rosie, Rosie, Rosie," Akoman said. "And what do you expect to do with that?"

She knew he was referring to her weapon, but she could not bring herself to answer; her terror was debilitating.

"Please, child, put it away. There's a good girl."

For reasons she could not fathom, she did as was told, feeling as though it were someone else performing the action for her as she holstered her gun slowly.

The front door took another gigantic shunt. This time Rosie was certain she heard Scott and Wilson's voices on the other side of it.

Akoman laughed. "Good girl. Now. Go and play."

She screamed as he grabbed her from behind, lifted her clean into the air and flung her to one side of the hallway, where she crashed into and through one of the doors, and all the while he chuckled in his maniacal fashion.

23

Scott coughed as he got to his feet, unsteady and swaying a little. Dust circled the room from his heavy landing into the dimly-lit room – wherever the hell he was – and it irritated his throat. As he strained his eyes to try to make sense of his location, a feeling of dread pervaded his senses. The place seemed wrong and not what he had expected to find himself in, having forced his way through the front door with Wilson.

Kalisha, he thought as he glanced around, realizing he could not spot the doctor. He called out his name and strained his ears for any faint sounds. There was nothing.

Scott had been no stranger to extreme dangers; his C.I.A. role having provided many intense situations in the past, but this was different. This was something he neither understood nor felt he could control, and it bothered him a great deal. When infiltrating an enemy cell or camp or tracking an enemy destined for execution, he had known the risks, having studied the target and evaluated the terrain. He knew how to manipulate all factors to best serve his needs, to get the job done with as little risk to his own life as possible. And he was no stranger to overwhelming forces, which is why he knew that the one now hunting him and Rosie was too much for them and way out of their league. With no intel or observations to work on, he had no idea how to defeat the demon, so he desperately needed to find Rosie and Kalisha, and fast.

"Where the hell am I?" he said as he reached into his jacket pocket and took out a small Maglite torch and turned it on. Guiding the beam around the room, he made out chains hanging from the roof of an open area in which various tools lay on workbenches. "A workshop?"

he said, as though speaking aloud might offer some comfort, so that he need not feel alone.

He contemplated the events leading up to him entering the house. The demon dogs had chased them down and split them up within the dense fog. He thought about the one that had nearly torn his throat out when it had launched at him and how, miraculously, he had somehow dodged the attack at the last second. He touched his throat, conscious of his luck. Had it been luck, though? Or had the demons been toying with them, herding them so that they were certain to make it inside the house at their master's behest?

He thought of how he found himself literally running into Kalisha, and how they had both shrieked like little schoolgirls – to hell with machoism; he would have no problem describing what had happened if he ever recounted the story. He frowned, thinking how they had joined shoulders to try to force the door open, having found it locked; the terrifying beasts snarling toward them within the thick fog. They had put all their weight into a combined and forceful shunt and Scott had grunted hard as the door had crashed open far more easily than he had anticipated, given its size and stature. Had they burst it open, or had it opened of its own accord? He couldn't be sure. He tried to think back: had they actually connected with the door? But the memory had drifted so far to the back of his mind he wondered if he might ever get it back again.

And then he had found himself here, in a room that smelled of dust and oil. As he struggled again to retrieve the memory of whether the door had opened by itself, a different one invaded his mind. As he had fallen through the door, he had been convinced that he had seen Rosie held aloft by Akoman, who had then thrown her to one side. But had he imagined that? Because this workshop was not that room, and not where he had thought he had landed. There was no Akoman, no Rosie and no Kalisha either.

"Goddammit!" he said as he walked forward slowly, careful not to bump into or be tripped by anything. For some reason, the workshop felt familiar, as though he had been there before – but that was impossible, as he had never been to this part of the state, let alone this house. Still, an overwhelming familiarity gnawed away at him, and he was unable to shake it.

A noise from the other side of the room made his spin to direct his attention toward it. He reached for and drew his firearm, then turned his torch so that it was held in his left fist and rested his weapon above it on his forearm, the torch lighting the path of his aim.

"Who's there?" he commanded, though he was still unable to shake the fear in his voice. "I'm an F.B.I. agent and I am armed. Show yourself."

He was well aware that it might be Akoman or one of his demons skulking in the darkness, but this is what he did and who he was, and if he allowed his identity as a law enforcement officer to succumb to fear, he might as well just give up and let them kill him.

"I repeat, I am an F.B.I. agent and I am armed. Whoever is there, come out with your hands in the air, then get down on the ground." Allowing himself to consider how ridiculous maintaining this façade was under these circumstances, he grunted. "For fuck's sake, Denver. Stupid. Stupid, stupid. No demon is gonna come out with its fucking hands in the air," he whispered to himself. He took a deep breath and edged his way forward to the point where the room opened up wider. At the back of the room, an overhead light turned on, with the accompanying sound of a toggle switch being pulled.

"Who's there?" he demanded again, wincing at the same time.

A figure shuffled toward the light but not quite into it, and he could only make out its basic form.

A broken, whispered, voice of a young female rasped from the darkness. "You didn't save me."

Scott strained his eyes and leaned toward the voice a little. "Hello? Who's there?"

"You didn't save me. You left me to die."

"Okay," he said, his brow furrowed. "F.B.I. – come out with your hands in the air and then get down on the ground in front of me."

The sly and hissing voice continued; this time accompanied by a shuffling sound. "You let him do this to me. You let him do this… to me."

Something gnawed inside him, telling him that this place was familiar, that he had been here before, and that feeling of recognition was growing and becoming much more powerful all the time.

"I know this place," he said, his eyes narrowed.

"You let him do this to me. You could have saved me, but you didn't. And now he plays with me down here, every single day. You did this to me."

"I know this place. I know this place. I've been here before." He lowered his weapon and torch a little.

The shuffling sound grew closer and then a shadowy figure slinked under the dim overhead light at the edge of his vision and he brought his gun back up instantly.

"You didn't look for me. You left me to die."

The voice changed from raspy to deep, demonic and aggressive. "YOU LEFT ME TO DIE."

Scott's anxiety grew as he cast torchlight around the room, noticing more objects that he recognized such as a distinctive looking old wood-furnace with a large red toolbox sat next to it, a stars and stripes mouth and tongue sticker of the band The Rolling Stones, affixed. "I've been here before. I have been in this room before."

The voice returned to the whispered, female version. "He did these things to me. Terrible things. He hurt me, and you let him. You did nothing to save me."

Scott looked down for a moment as a final piece of the puzzle slotted into place in his mind. "Bob Brannigan's workshop," he said. His gaze lifted to the shadowy figure. "Bob Brannigan's workshop, where we found Polly Marsh. This is where we found Polly Marsh." He took in a sharp breath. "This is where we found… you."

"YOU LEFT ME TO DIE!" the voice screamed again. "You left me to die and he did all those things to me."

Scott's lips trembled and heat ran up his neck. Again, he lowered his weapon, the torchlight tracing across the dirty, oil-stained floor, and tears welled in his eyes. "That's not true. THAT'S NOT TRUE! We looked for you. We did all we could to find you. We looked for you. *I* LOOKED FOR YOU!"

The shadowy figure moved at great speed from under the light to the other side of the room, startling him and making him bring his weapon back up to track its scampering movements.

"YOU LOOKED FOR ME?" it screamed.

The sound came from Scott's right rather than where he was currently looking, so he spun around, once more straining to look into the darkness. A light came on to his left, and again he quickly retrained his sights, his breathing becoming more erratic with each passing moment. Then the voice screamed from behind him, causing him to spin around and almost lose his footing.

"YOU LOOKED FOR ME?"

147

The figure was right in front of him. It was covered in a white sheet which was stained with blood. Scott reeled backward so fast that he stumbled and fell onto his backside, then frantically scrambled away. He attempted to regain his composure and raised his weapon to the sheeted figure, his hand trembling, then got to his feet quickly, gripping his weapon in both hands, the torch having skittered away when he fell. He wet his mouth, then forced out a few breaths through puckered lips in an attempt to regain control.

"You didn't want to find me," the figure continued. "You wanted him to do those things to me. You wanted him to kill me. You wanted him to fuck me. YOU WANTED HIM TO GUT ME! You... wanted... it."

Scott was close to tears, forced to relive the memory of how he found the body of 12-year-old Polly Marsh, one of the earliest and worst cases of his career at the agency and his first as lead agent. He had been desperate to find the girl; frantic, even. Not only in hoping to keep the promise he had made to the child's parents, and to prove to his peers and superiors that he was a capable addition to team, but somehow he had hoped that in saving her he could redeem himself in the eyes of whatever great power people prayed to, and therefore save his soul despite the terrible things he had done during his military career. He had tried everything to find Polly, and eventually he had learned where she was: Brannigan's workshop. But though time was of the essence, red tape and bureaucracy had inserted itself into the mix, as it often did, and by the time he and his team had secured the search warrant and found her, it had been too late. The things that Bob Brannigan had done to her had turned his stomach – and it was saying something for Scott Denver to be so disturbed.

Emotion overcame him and tears streaked down his cheeks. "That's not true, Polly. We did all we could to find you. I did all I could to find you and I *did* find you."

"But not in time, you fucking pig," she screamed. "You were more interested in your fucking career, more interested in getting in His good graces for murdering countless innocents. You never cared about me. Only yourself."

Scott frowned. How could she know that? Even if only part of it were true.

Polly started to move toward him, her pace slow and irregular, as though it pained her to move her stiff limbs. "And so what, pig? You found me. But how did that help me? He gutted me like a fish, stabbed me in my eyes as I screamed, all the while with his fucking dick inside me, hurting me, violating me. HOW DID THAT HELP ME?"

Scott backed away as the bloodied and sheeted figure of Polly Marsh staggered toward him. "I'm sorry," he said, almost sobbing, "I tried, really I tried, but we couldn't get the search warrant fast enough, The judge, he was… we couldn't get it fast enough, and I tried. He would've walked if I had gone in without it."

"But I would have been alive."

"I know," he said, this time giving into emotion and sobbing. "I know. But—"

"I WOULD HAVE BEEN ALIVE!" she screamed, then moved toward him at a faster pace, though her movements were still juddering and broken.

Scott screamed and stumbled backward, his back crashing into the large toolbox. He raised his arms in front of his face. Though he wasn't sure if what he was seeing was real or not, his bluff had been called and he wasn't been prepared to fire a round into the corpse of Polly Marsh; that would have been too much for him. He cried out again as she came to a halt right in front of him and stood motionless. He tried to get his breathing under control as he slowly lowered his arms and stared at the form under the bloody sheet. Despite his abject terror and every fiber in his body yelling at him not to, he felt an unwavering need to see underneath the sheet, to know it was her. He couldn't explain it, nor could he help it, but nevertheless he reached out to the sheet slowly, his hand trembling. The air chilled and she saw breath permeate the sheet, subtle at first but then growing denser with each breath until it resembled thick smoke from a cigar. His hand continued to shake as he bunched the sheet within his fist. Closing his eyes for a moment, he then pulled at the sheet and it fell away.

There was nothing there. No Polly Marsh, no creature or demon. Nothing.

He sobbed and let go of the sheet, then bent double with his hands on his knees, attempting to compose himself. "Fuck. Fuck, fuck, fuck, fuck. It's not real. It's not real. She's not real."

He returned to a standing position. Behind him, crouched atop the toolbox, grinned a naked Polly; her face and skin patchworked together after the carnage and mutilation wrought upon her by Bob Brannigan.

"Are you sure, Scott?" she rasped into his ear.

He cried out and reeled onto all fours, scrambling to the other side of the room, where he turned back around to see Polly let herself fall from the toolbox, her face hitting the concrete with a sickening thud. She inched her head upward to stare at him, a crazed grin on her face. Her limbs moved slowly in circles, over one another, unnatural as though she were a plastic doll. She inched toward him, streaks of her blood trailing behind her. Scott scrambled away from the terrifying sight, but she gained momentum and speed, her body creaking and cracking as it moved.

He gave into fear and unloaded his weapon into Polly's advancing form, a final act of desecration to ensure his own survival. From each bullet hole ejected spurts of blood, but she continued to grin at him and cackle as her speed increased and she bore down on him, undeterred.

Out of bullets, and nearing the limits of his sanity, Scott Denver screamed and put his hands in front of his face as Polly Marsh's mutilated body shrieked at him.

24

Wilson picked himself up from the floor of the entrance to the manor, then turned quickly back to face the door he had just crashed through. He was expecting to see Scott doing the same, picking himself up and dusting himself down, but he was alone. He called out Scott's name, but there was no reply – eerily, there was no sound of any description, not even an echo. He frowned, then called out again, this time to Rosie, but as before, nothing. He contemplated the events outside the manor as he gripped the old brown satchel slung across his body, feeling its contents from the outside to ensure that nothing seemed broken.

"What am I dealing with here?" he said.

One thing that Wilson Kalisha valued highly was his ability to remember even the tiniest of details and, in turn, to use that information to help others. It was his memory that had served him so well in assisting those who came to him, listening to what they had to say, remembering each and every detail so that the information presented could be used immediately, should he discern even a flicker of similarity to other events. He was able to perform such tasks without the need to take notes, such was the eidetic nature of his memory. In short, he was absolute in his recollection of what he had just witnessed.

Before he and Scott had offered the final and decisive shunt to open the door, he had caught a glimpse of Rosie racing toward them through the fog, a demon giving chase and close behind her. Being linked to Scott, who had pulled him through, Wilson had not had enough time to try to assist her – however, his mind had reeled as, upon falling into the entrance hall, he had seen Akoman holding Rosie aloft and grinning before tossing her aside. When Wilson had crashed to the floor he had looked up but had seen no sign of the demon nor Rosie, and the door into she had been flung and she had smashed through was open and still intact.

He spun on his heels as, to the right side of the staircase and along a small, narrow passageway, a door crashed open. He heard raised voices.

He took a deep breath.

One voice was Scott's. The other... his own.

25

Rosie cried out in great pain as she crashed through the door and tumbled into something hard and metallic, hitting her head. She reached up to her forehead to feel a nasty gash, and her fingers came away wet. She looked up and back to the door she had come through to see it now closed, then blinked as she tried to make sense of where she was. Gingerly, she raised herself to her feet and winced: putting weight onto her foot felt sore. She sat down, without even thinking what it was she had sat upon. She looked down to see it was a bed, a basic yet functional iron-framed unit covered in a skanky-looking patchwork quilt and with stained and dirty pillows. As she brought her foot up and crossed it over her other leg to rub it, she took in the rest of her surroundings. The room was dirty, with bare wooden floorboards and ripped and peeling floral wallpaper that seemed more appropriate for a home in the 70s. She glanced to a window to her left as multicolored light flashed, making the room glow with one color and another, enhancing the sleazy vibe.

"Where the fuck am I?" she said. She took a deep breath and continued to examine the room.

Without warning, the door she had come through burst open, startling her. A man and girl stumbled in. The man was laughing but the girl was not; her face was somber and pained. They shuffled toward the bed, making Rosie leap to her feet, hopping slightly as the pain in her ankle flared again. She moved to one side so as not to be hit by them, as they seemed oblivious to her presence.

Rosie's eyes widened and her jaw dropped as she recognized the man. "Daddy?" she said, frowning. Her father didn't acknowledge her.

Instead, he began groping at the young girl. Rosie's hand shot to her mouth and tears filled her eyes.

The young girl stared over her father's shoulder at Rosie with a doleful expression. She did not resist the aggressive pawing she was being subjected to. Instead, she kept her vacant gaze fixed, as though staring into another time and place.

"Stop. STOP!" Rosie cried. She strode over to her father and grabbed him by the collar and yanked it, attempting to pull him off the child.

Her father grabbed her shirt, bunching it in his fist, then turned his gaze toward her while pulling her down to his eyeline. "What are you doing here, peanut? You shouldn't be here. This is Daddy's time. This is so I don't have to do these things to you, peanut." He pushed her forcefully, sending her crashing backward into a cabinet. Then he returned to molesting the child.

"STOP THIS. STOP IT NOW!" Rosie demanded, and began to move toward him again. She stopped abruptly as her father's head whipped around to face her, immense anger burning in his eyes.

"You shouldn't be here, Rosie. This is my time. MY TIME." His voice grew deeper. "You're not welcome here, peanut. Why are you spying on Daddy?" His voice boomed, becoming deeper still and taking on a demonic tone. "Why are you spying on your daddy?" He stood, then looked down at the child, who continued to stare blankly at Rosie. Then he punched the girl in the face, hard. Her nose exploded, blood spraying outward as her head rocked backward then rebounded. Her expression remained unchanged. "Why are you spying on me?" he said again. He punched the child a second time, this time shattering her jaw. Her head flopped down and lolled to one side.

Rosie screamed for him to stop and then she attacked him, but once more he pushed her with immense force, sending her crashing into the wall to one side of the door.

"I do these things to her so I don't have to do them to you," he said, his voice now fully demonic. He turned to the young girl and continued to hit her. The child's expression and demeanor still did not change, as though each blow had no effect on her despite the physical damage. Rosie's father roared and turned back to face her. "Is it for that cunt of a mother of yours? Are you spying for her?"

Rosie sobbed and sagged against the wall. "Please. Stop. Stop. This isn't real. This is a lie."

Her father's voice became high-pitched as he mimicked her. "Please. Stop. This is a lie."

He shot toward her in a blur and slammed both his hands against the wall to either side of her head, making her jump and cry out in fright.

"You think your mother is soooo righteous, that she's soooo innocent. But you don't know her like I know her. She's a dirty whore. A dirty, priest-fucking whore. She's with him right now, you know – sucking his cock, taking it in the ass. Nasty, dirty shit. She's trash, and she's made *you* trash as well."

He rose into the air slightly, and floated backward rapidly, his toes pointing down and scraping against the wooden floorboards.

He pointed at the child. "I do this to her so I don't have to do it to you. Can't you see that?" His face began to display signs of burning, his skin smoking and becoming blistered. "But she burns as well. Just like me, she burns in Hell." He laughed, deep and demonic. "She burns in Hell and the priest burns with her. And they burn, and they fuck; and they fuck, and they burn." He roared with laughter, throwing his head back. The young girl joined in, her stare still fixed firmly on Rosie. Her laughter turned to screams as her face began melting, as did Rosie's father's, yet still, the girl's gaze remained fixated upon Rosie and she smiled through her screams.

The room filled with smoke, though there was no sign of any fire, and as their screams reached a crescendo, the child stood and advanced toward Rosie, alongside her father.

Rosie scrambled along the wall toward the door and began tugging frantically at the handle in an attempt to open it.

"We all burn down here," her father screamed, followed by pained laughter that was copied by the child. He continued to inch toward Rosie. "We all burn and soon, so shall you all. This world will soon know His triumph – will soon know what it is like to bathe in the blood of their own madness. They will know pain. They will know torture. They *will* know Hell." He opened his mouth to reveal rows of demonic, blood-stained teeth.

Then he lunged at Rosie.

Unable to open the door, Rosie ceased trying as her screaming father pounced upon her. She raised her arms in front of her face as protection.

Nothing happened. He hadn't grabbed her. As she slowly opened her eyes and dropped her arms, she saw that she was no longer in the sleazy hotel room.

She glanced around. She was in her mom and dad's old bedroom. Her eyes narrowed and darted from side to side. She turned around quickly at the sound of the bedroom door opening, but no one came through it. She turned back to look at her parents' bed, then reacted with shock and disgust to see her mother and the family priest completely naked and engaged in sex, her mother on all fours and the priest taking her from behind. Rosie sobbed and once again raised her hands to her mouth.

Her mother ceased moaning and turned to look at Rosie while the priest continued to thrust and groan. She smiled. "His house visits are always so… enlightening."

Rosie shook her head as tears cascaded down her cheeks. Then she gasped as the priest's head turned all the way around, creaking and cracking, while he continued his intercourse with her mother.

"I fucking love your family, Rosie," he said with a salacious grin. "It's your turn next, my child." He started to laugh as he continued to stare at her, his lewd expression turning darker and more menacing as his thrusts into Rosie's mom grew increasingly aggressive. His laughter grew in intensity and then his face morphed into that of Akoman.

Rosie jolted and hurried to the open bedroom door. Akoman's demonic laughter roared in her ears as she stepped through, slamming the door shut and resting her back against it, then sliding down it in floods of tears.

26

Wilson crept through the door and into a huge and grand, but derelict, L-shaped banquet hall. A wood-paneled wall to his right stretched a little way into the room preventing him from seeing it in its entirety. What he could see was a gigantic chandelier that hung over the center of the room and seemed in uncharacteristically good condition compared to the rest of the room. He gasped as he caught sight of himself kneeling underneath the ornate decoration, in the center of what appeared to be large pentagram drawn in what he could only assume was blood, given its dark reddish-brown color. He took a few steps forward into the room as his other self cried out in distress.

"Stay away from me, demon. You stay away," his doppelganger said.

Wilson inched forward as he placed a hand on the wood paneling that obscured his full view of the banquet hall and peeked around the corner to see who his other self was speaking to.

On the other side of the room, Scott was slowly advancing toward the other Wilson, his weapon drawn but at his side, his other hand held out in a placating gesture.

"Hey. HEY!" Scott shouted, then raised his weapon with both hands, aimed at the kneeling Wilson. "Doctor. Doctor Kalisha. It's me, it's Agent Denver. Please, put the knife down. I don't want to hurt you."

It was only now that Wilson realized his counterpart was holding a large kitchen knife and had raised it to Scott.

"What is going on here?" Wilson said, frowning and taking a couple more steps forward. "What in the name of God is happening?"

27

Rosie entered another room, one completely bare and devoid of furniture. She was lost, with no clue where to go or what to do, and her anxiety was rising by the second. Her head flopped forward and she sighed. She turned to walk out of the room but stopped as Larry's ethereal voice called to her from behind.

"You did this. This is all your fault."

She spun on her heels, drawing and raising her weapon and pointing it ahead of her. There was nothing there; the room was still empty. Her breathing raced and her eyes darted from side to side in her certainty that something would scream and race toward her out of nothingness to terrify her.

She wiped her brow, removing the sweat that had beaded upon it, and groaned. Her stress levels were the highest they had ever been, and she wasn't sure how much more of it she could take. The anxiety was damaging her, and she could no longer be sure how long she had been in the house. At best, she figured it had been a few hours, but the toll of the exhaustion she felt was telling her otherwise: that it could have been much, much longer. She had checked the time on her phone a few times, but the time was locked at 09:47, which she knew could not be right, not to mention she had no signal whatsoever.

Larry's ghostly voice sounded from behind her again, bringing her back into the moment. She reeled around but, as before, he wasn't there. Then she heard a scratching sound to her left and turned toward it quickly, to see him standing in the corner of the room, facing the wall and scratching at it with his fingers. She raised her gun. "Larry?" she said, slowly advancing on him. She grunted. "No, of course not. It's not you. This is just one of his little tricks. And I am getting sick of this bullshit."

Larry chuckled. "Brave, brave, brave, brave, brave. You always had to be the brave one, Rosie. But if you hadn't been so brave, then maybe I would still be alive. Maybe." He continued to scratch at the wall and chuckle, but now he began to sway. "Brave little Rosie Hendricks. Brave, brave, brave."

He repeated the word over and over as she approached him, although the words lessened in volume each time until his voice was nothing more than a whisper.

"Yeah," she said, reaching out to him, "I'm real brave, Larry. So why don't you be brave too, and show me your face?"

He stopped repeating the word, and ceased swaying. "You want to see my face?" He chuckled, then slowly began to turn. Rosie held her breath and gripped her gun tight, wondering if it had been a bad idea to get him to reveal his face to her. She wet her mouth and swallowed hard, her breathing becoming deeper and sweat building up again on her forehead. But just before Larry turned to face her completely, he vanished before her eyes.

Rosie froze and her eyes darted, her senses warning her that something was coming.

"BRAVE!" Larry screamed from right behind her, thrusting his mutilated face over her shoulder and making Rosie scream and stumble forward.

She fell into the wall, hard, then turned around while almost sliding down it. She raised her weapon to him. She sobbed, her face contorted with equal parts terror and grief at the sight of Larry's horrifically butchered form.

He laughed maniacally as he grabbed at his face and clawed it, gouging chunks of flesh from it and allowing gore to plop to the floor beneath him.

"You did this to me," he shrieked, "this is your fault and now I suffer daily for your sins. Just like your fucking evil father and your filthy whore mother."

Larry shambled to and dropped to his knees in front of her as she slid further down the wall, recoiling at the sight of him, her gun close to her chest. His face was so close to hers that it was almost touching, making her close her eyes.

"We all suffer down here, Rosie. And you will too, you fucking bitch. Once he completes the ritual, once he finishes his mission and unleashes the Morning Star's fury, then you and all the others will suffer in beautiful, agonizing ecstasy. But your Hell will be here, above and not below as mine is." He scampered backward on all fours, all the while grinning at her. "His time has come. Not long now. He will reign. He is risen!"

Rosie's eyes snapped open and she gritted her teeth, raising her gun in a desperate attempt to control her all-consuming terror.

Larry cackled, making an awful clicking sound. "And what do you intend to do? Kill me? I'm already fucking dead, you stupid cunt, remember."

She was losing control of her sanity and the harder she tried to hold onto it, the further it seemed to slip away. She shook her head in exasperation as Larry's cackling continued. Her weapon lowered slightly. She started and raised it again, and followed Larry as he scurried away like a spider, crawling up the wall at the opposite side of the room to hang in the corner. She cried out in fright and her breathing became erratic at the creepiness of his actions, and tears spilled down her cheeks.

"But since we were such friends," he continued, turning his head to look at her, "I'll feed you some good intel. Get you a leg up in the game, so to speak."

She shook her head and inhaled a shaky breath. "I don't want any more lies from you. You're not my partner, you're not Larry, and you are not my friend. I don't know what the hell you are, but Larry would never do this to me." She grew a little braver – and angrier – although she was still sobbing. "So go back to your fucking master, you creepy bastard, or so help me God, I will unload every last round in this gun into you."

The creature roared with laughter. "Go ahead, bitch. I'm dead, *remember.*"

She gritted her teeth and her finger tensed on the trigger.

"But I wouldn't waste them if I were you," he said, still laughing. "I would save them for your real threat."

She huffed, exasperated and angry. "What are you talking about? The fuck do you mean by that?"

He cackled again. "You think you know everything about everyone, but your 'knowledge' is severely misguided. Take your new friend,

Agent Denver." He grinned, sly and sickening. "Do you really know all there is to know about him?"

Her eyes narrowed. "Fuck off with this shit. I told you, no more lies. I don't wanna hear anymore bullshit from you. No more lies."

He mimicked her like a parrot. "No more lies. No more lies." He laughed again. "Interesting you would say that, since you've been fed a web of lies since you first met him."

His words caused her to glance down but the moment she did, she looked back up at him, worried that taking her eyes off him for any amount of time would spell her doom.

"As powerful a demon my master Akoman is, he still requires… *lackeys* in this realm." He cackled. "Help is always… appreciated." He grinned, then ran his long tongue over his lips and made noises of gratification. "Help is always appreciated, Rosie."

Abruptly, his form disintegrated into thousands of spiders that cascaded to the floor and scurried toward her.

Rosie scrambled to her feet with a scream and ran to the door.

28

Wilson strode forward, further into the banquet hall as his doppelganger squared off against Scott. He jumped in fright as Rosie crashed down onto a table from above and then rolled off it, holding her ribs and groaning. Both his other self and Scott turned to look at her as she scrambled back onto her feet, grimacing.

Wilson frowned as Rosie raised her weapon to Scott.

"Stay right there, Denver. Don't you fucking move," she said.

"Rosie, what the hell are you doing? It's me," Scott replied, his weapon still pointed at the other Kalisha, whose confused attention flitted between the two of them.

"Wait. Wait!" Wilson – the Wilson who had just entered the room – said to the three of them. He staggered forward, but they didn't seem to hear him. Suddenly, he felt unwell and stumbled. Something ran down his forehead and he moved his hand to it; feeling wetness, he lowered it to see that his hand was covered in blood. He looked up, his eyes narrowed, and saw Akoman standing next to his other self, who was kneeling in the center of the pentagram. The demon looked directly at him then cocked his head to one side, stuck out his bottom lip and rubbed his eyes with his knuckles in a mockery of crying.

"Oh, God. Oh, God, no," Wilson said, then took a deep breath. "I'm dead."

"Yes. You are," Akoman said from behind him, startling him and making him spin around, unsteady on his feet. "You are dead, dear Dr Kalisha. I killed you hours ago but I thought it would be amusing to bring you to this moment before you slip away and leave for the White Kingdom – a Heaven that will soon be destroyed by my master. You see, dear Dr Kalisha, it will amuse me greatly to have you watch these final moments before I kill you… two hours ago, that is." He grinned. "A real mindfuck, no?" He chuckled. "This thing is done. You have all lost." He placed a clawed hand on top of the confused man's head and turned it to face the show. "Now watch. And enjoy."

Akoman smiled and licked his lips.

29

Rosie screamed as she turned a corner at the end of a corridor and bumped into Scott. She pushed him away quickly, drawing and raising her gun.

"Whoa, Rosie. It's me. It's me, it's Scott."

She didn't lower her weapon, instead wrapping both hands around it and keeping it firmly trained on him.

"Hey, it's me. Rosie. What the fuck!" he said, frowning and taking a step forward.

Rosie thrust her firearm toward him a little, signifying her serious intent.

Scott threw his hands into the air and ceased his advance. "Okay. Okay. Let's just calm down here."

"Who are you, Denver?" she asked, "Who the fuck... are you?"

Scott lowered his hands into a placatory gesture and spoke softly. "Okay, detective. Take it easy. I'm sure you have experienced some bad shit in here, the same as me, but you are being toyed with. The demon is messing with us. Get a grip and think like the rational police officer that you are." He took a step toward her, one hand outstretched.

"Don't move. Don't you fucking move," she said.

Scott stopped and sighed. "Rosie. Come on. Think, will ya? This is all part of his game."

She stared at him for a few moments as he raised his eyebrows and pursed his lips, his hands still raised in pacification. Finally, she sighed heavily, then lowered her weapon and looked at the ground, shaking her head.

"Atta girl," he said with a smile. He took a step toward her. "Thank God you saw sense."

She nodded and pushed past him, continuing along the corridor in the same direction as before.

"Good," Scott said from behind her. "Now let's go find that fucking doctor and we can end him, once and for all."

She frowned and stopped, then slowly turned back to face him.

"And then, Rosie, maybe the visions of your stupid, dead fucking parents will stop."

Her eyes widened. "What? What did you just say?"

His face contorted into a menacing grin. "I said, maybe you will stop being a whiny little bitch and you can let your shitty, dead fucking parents rest in peace, you selfish little fuck."

She snapped her weapon back up to him as his grin widened, stretching across his face almost from ear to ear.

He began to laugh, and his voice turned more demonic with each word he uttered. "Oh, Rosie, Rosie, Rosie. It's time, my dear Rosie. It's finally time. He will reign. He is risen!" He looked upward and stretched out his arms in praise.

Rosie stared in horror as his clothes split as though a knife had been run up them. They fell to the ground and then his skin, too, began to shed, peeling and cascading down as he transformed into a jackal demon. The face of a terrifying beast pushed through Scott's human features, splitting and tearing as a huge snout cracked and crunched forward. A horrifying mouth filled with sharp teeth opened beneath it, spittle and saliva spraying and dripping onto the ground. The demon then thrust its arms to the sides and opened its clawed fingers, wiggling them as it stared at Rosie through burning yellow eyes and cackled.

Rosie shot four times into the demon's chest. Although the creature rocked with each impact, she realized that the gunfire was having little effect.

The demon chuckled again and looked down at the wounds that oozed black liquid. "It's time to finish this. Run, little piggy. Run, run."

Rosie spun on her heels and bolted as the demon roared and charged after her. She grunted in terror as she sensed it close in. It was almost upon her, therefore she decided to try the first door she came to on her right. She was in luck: the door swung open. She turned quickly and shoved it closed just as the demon pounded into it, preventing her from closing it fully. She cried out in fright, putting all her strength into trying to shut it.

The demon's snout thrust through the gap, and she beat at it with her weapon, trying to force it to retreat. She knew it was pointless; the creature was too powerful and would soon force the door open. She had to do something as the barrage was escalating, so she looked around quickly to see that she was standing on a balcony overlooking a large hall. Her eyes widened as, on the ground, she saw Wilson kneeling in the center of a large pentagram. He held a knife in both hands, pointing it at something that she could not see.

She heard an exchange between him and Scott.

"Stay away from me, demon. You stay away," Kalisha said, his voice trembling along with his knife-wielding hands.

"Hey. HEY! Doctor. Doctor Kalisha. It's me – it's Agent Denver. Please, put the knife down. I don't want to hurt you."

The pounding at the door intensified, and it began to open further. With a scream, Rosie let go and ran, and the door smashed open to reveal the demon in pursuit.

Without a second thought, she leapt over the balcony with a scream and dropped down fifteen feet, landing onto a table that buckled and splintered under her weight. Pain shot through her knees and into her ribs, making her grunt in agony – but to her eternal gratitude, she had managed to keep hold of her weapon. With adrenaline coursing through her, she got to her feet quickly. She snapped her attention to the balcony above, expecting to see the demon leap over and come crashing down on her, but it did not. There was nothing there.

She rounded on Wilson, who was kneeling on the floor, and then looked up at Scott, who stared back at her, his mouth agape and his weapon raised to the doctor. He then glanced up to the balcony from which she had jumped, then back to her. He seemed about to say something when she raised her gun to him and said, "Stay right there, Denver. Don't you fucking move."

Scott frowned hard. "Rosie, what the hell are you doing? It's me," he said, though he kept his weapon trained on Kalisha.

She shook her head and ran her tongue over her bottom lip. "You said that a minute ago before you changed into a fucking creature and tried to rip me apart. No more lies, Denver. Put the fucking gun down and don't even think about changing into that thing."

"Rosie," Scott shouted, his eyes wide, "have you lost your goddamn mind? It's me – it's Scott." His eyes darted left and right. "You're being fucked with. It's Akoman. He's fucking with all of us. I've just spent the last few hours pursued by corpses from my old cases, and people I have put in the fucking ground during missions. It's not real. He's toying with us. Don't you see? This is how he works. This is what he does."

Rosie shook her head, but Scott's words began to have some effect on her. "But…" she said, looking down at the ground as if searching for answers at her feet.

"Rosie. *Think*. Akoman's got us pitched against one another, having fucked with our minds for hours so that we don't know what's up or what's down. Don't fall for it."

She looked up at him again, her mouth opening and closing when, from above and behind the chandelier, Akoman descended slowly to the ground, his soulless, perpetual grin at its most menacing. He landed just behind the sobbing Dr Kalisha, who was shaking, wracked with terror.

Akoman smiled. "And so. We are finally here. At the end." He roared with demonic laughter.

Rosie shifted her aim to Akoman, who glanced at her and grinned. Then he turned toward Scott.

"It's time to fulfill your promise, Agent Denver. Time to fulfill your destiny. Murder them both so that His will can be done and Lucifer's reign upon this world can begin."

Rosie snapped her weapon back to Scott.

"Hey, HEY!" Scott said, holding up a hand to her. "Do not listen to this fucking thing. It is lying. He is lying to you. Rosie. Listen to me."

"Do it, Scott," Akoman demanded. "Do it and fulfill your promise. Do it."

Rosie began to sob. "Denver. Please, put your gun down."

Scott took a deep breath. "Detective Sergeant Rosie Hendricks, do not listen to this creature. You are an officer of the law. Think, will ya? This is all part of his game."

Rosie shook her head, tears trickling down her cheeks. Her mind was spinning. She wasn't sure what was real or what was fake anymore. Her terror had overwhelmed her, and she didn't know what to do. She just wanted to go home, to forget that this had ever happened, that she had seen any of the things she had. Even more, she wanted to go back in time, to before the case of the first victim landed on her desk, to when she and Larry were happy; spending weekends away at secret rendezvous or taking romantic walks in beautiful locations. She wanted Larry back and she wanted all of this to go away.

She closed her eyes. "You said that already, Scott. You said that just before you changed into a demon. I don't know what to believe anymore."

"Believe me, Rosie. Believe me and know that I will not hurt you, or Kalisha. There is no need for you to think about defending yourself. We need to band together and defeat this fucking demon. Together."

Akoman laughed. "Scott. Stop. The game is over. We have won. No need to drag this out. Kill them."

Wilson got to his feet, his shoulders heaving and his breathing deep and erratic.

Scott's attention flitted between Wilson and Rosie as the witch doctor began to shake and make groaning noises.

"Doctor," Scott shouted, "get a grip, man. Fight this."

Kalisha's grunting became more pronounced and his breathing became even more erratic. His eyes widened.

Scott raised his gun to him, his posture hardening. "Dr Kalisha, I am warning you. Get a hold of yourself and put the knife down. NOW!"

"You will not take me, demon," Wilson screamed. He charged at Scott, slashing the knife from side to side.

"STOP!" Scott screamed.

"You will not trick me as you did before, ungodly beast," Kalisha shouted, increasing his speed.

Scott fired one shot and Wilson dropped to the ground.

Two shots exploded, and Scott slumped to the floor.

Akoman laughed. "It is done."

Rosie breathed hard. She felt dizzy. She looked at Akoman for a moment, then to the point where Wilson had fallen – but there was no sign of him, so her attention returned swiftly to Scott.

"No, no, no, no, no," she said as she ran over to him, scrambling onto her knees at his side. She turned him over and called his name, but his lifeless expression told her he was dead.

She screamed. With tear-filled eyes, she rested her head against his forehead and whispered, "I'm sorry. I'm so, so sorry. What have I done? Oh my God, I'm lost, I'm so lost. I don't know what is happening anymore."

"Well. That's that, then." Akoman said, walking to her side and causing her to drop Scott's body and scramble away, her gun raised. "Just need to put this one with the other and we're done."

Rosie looked past him, to the pentagram. Wilson's naked and mutilated corpse was held in position with railway spikes, like all of the previous victims. Her attention then snapped to Scott's body as Akoman clicked his fingers and Scott's clothing ripped away from him as though pulled by unseen forces. Next, Akoman rammed a knife into Scott's belly and slit him open to his neck. Rosie cried out and raised a hand to her mouth, her sobbing growing more intense. She closed her eyes and looked away. Akoman's serrating action disturbed her so much that she was only able to reopen them when the sound of cutting had ceased.

The demon then tossed the knife to one side and reached into the wound. He removed Scott's heart with one hand, then clicked the fingers of his free hand, causing Scott's body to slide across the floor toward the pentagram. Rosie turned away, unable to look as Scott's head lolled to one side. It had seemed as though he was staring at her, judging her.

As Scott's body reached Kalisha's side, it underwent a sickening series of limb and bone breakages, his arms dislocating and wrenching across his back, his hands joining across his buttocks. Then a large railway spike materialized from thin air and slammed down into the hands and through the coccyx. Next, the body flipped over quickly, the legs dislocated at the hips and splayed outwards. Once again, railway spikes appeared from nowhere and slammed into his feet, nailing them to the floor.

Still holding Scott's heart, Akoman strode over to Rosie and knelt beside her, smiling. "If it's any consolation, I killed that so-called witch doctor hours ago and it wasn't even fun; quite boring, actually. Not like it was with you and Agent Denver. Thank you for your cooperation. I had a great time. But now? Well, now I need to finish this so I can get some much-needed rest. Been busy-busy of late." He chuckled.

Rosie grunted defiantly and raised her gun to her head. "You fucker. You won't win. I won't let you win. You need to kill me as the eighteenth victim to complete your ritual. Well… fuck you. I'll do it myself and deny you that right."

She squeezed the trigger.

Nothing happened.

She tried again, and again, but still, no shot.

Akoman gave an impatient smile. "You pathetic monkeys." He grabbed the gun from her. "You think you have all the answers. You think you know how everything works. I make the rules in here, Rosie. I won't be letting you kill yourself. I want you to see the fruits of our labors." He stood and walked away from her, then glanced back. "Clever girl, though, for figuring out that suicide would fuck up my claim to a victim. Clever, clever girl."

Rosie looked down and sobbed, then screamed and looked up at him. "You need eighteen victims. You need eighteen."

"And I have them." Akoman retorted, rounding on her. His glare softened, although his demeanor was still terrifying. "My dear Rosie. I will give you and Agent Denver credit for figuring out the three blocks of six connection. But the reality of it is not what you envisioned, nor are your conclusions correct, my dear." He returned to Scott's and Kalisha's bodies. "I didn't need to kill eighteen worthless and pathetic humans; I only needed seventeen for the summoning. The final part was an unwilling executioner." He smiled and knelt beside Scott's mangled corpse. "Thank you, Rosie, for murdering poor, dear innocent Agent Denver here." He chuckled. "He was right – you did do my work for me and you did it to perfection, my child. History has regularly failed to record my antics correctly and it had always been written: eighteen victims, eighteen murders. Not so, my dear. Not so at all." He grinned. "I make the rules, remember!"

Rosie could handle no more. She slumped to the ground, sobbing. Was this real? Was it over? Had Akoman won and had they lost? She felt trapped in a nightmare from which she could not wake, though a strong part of her screamed that none of this was happening, that it was just another of the demon's illusions and that very soon she would wake in her bed, safe and sound, and this would all be over. But the rational part of her – of what little rationality was left – told her otherwise, that where she was right now was a hell of her own making, and if Akoman was to be believed, she had been responsible for what was about to happen. She felt sickness rising within her, bubbling up her throat. She couldn't hold it in. She threw up, retching harder than she had ever done before in her life.

Akoman glanced at Scott's body once more, then stood and smiled. "In a few moments, his bidding will be done, and this will mark the start of his reign. All those unable to resist his influence will fall, he will secure the child, and then, the human world. The apocalypse starts here."

Rosie dragged herself to her feet, sniffing and wiping her nose with the back of her hand.

Akoman laughed and nodded a couple of times. "I will allow you to leave this place, Rosie. I will allow you to leave and witness firsthand the wonders and beautiful terrors that await you out there. I think that is only fair, for the mother of the end of days. My kin will be so happy to meet you… before they rip you apart."

Akoman moved into the center of the pentagram and raised the hand holding Scott's heart. He closed his eyes and muttered a few inaudible words, then reopened them and bit into the heart, blood spurting from it and running down his chin. He devoured the whole thing, then slammed his bloodied hand onto the ground and screamed another series of incantations.

Rosie jumped at the sound of cracking and splintering concrete. Scott's and Kalisha's bodies began to circle the edge of the pentagram, slowly at first but then gathering speed and momentum. Her attention snapped to Akoman as he continued to chant, the words loud and foul-sounding to her ears. The cyclone of spinning bodies added to the horrific noise, and the ground and building began to shake. Chunks of masonry fell from above and crashed to the ground around her, making her jump and scream.

Akoman had gotten to his feet and was enveloped in a whirling sea of red light. He cackled at her maniacally. "Run, run little piggy. Time to go. Run, run, run."

A thunderous series of booming sounds erupted from the center of the demonic ritual. Rosie felt them rip through not only her body but also her soul, as images flashed in front of her eyes: the earth, totally destroyed and demonic creatures roaming the land, killing everything in sight. People lay dead in the streets, their bodies mutilated and butchered beyond recognition. Others were hoisted on inverted crosses, their insides spilling from their bodies and slapping onto the floor.

"RUN, RUN NOW, LITTLE PIGGY," Akoman screamed at her.

Rosie jolted into life as the building began to disintegrate all around her. She raced to an open door at the far end, where beams of light poured through as though lighting her evacuation route. As she hurtled toward it, she cried out in terror, dodging the rubble that fell all around her and throwing her hands up to protect herself.

Careering through the doorway, she raced into the entrance hallway to the manor just as the front door exploded open and off its hinges. She ran through and outside, into the cool early-evening air. Behind her, the house crumbled and broke. The noise was deafening as the demolition neared its completion.

Still running, Rosie glanced back to see a huge tear open in the ground, swallowing what was left of the mansion. She screamed and continued to sprint away as it tracked its way toward her. The ground jolted beneath her, causing her to stumble, and she fell over with a painful thud, then turned onto her back and scrambled away from the expanding fissure. To her great relief, the encroaching chasm finally stopped widening. The remains of the house slipped into it, gone forever.

Rosie Hendricks panted as she sat alone; face dirty and bleeding, hands and arms covered in bruises, and she cried harder than she had before in her life.

What had she done? What terrible nightmares had she wrought on the world?

The 'message received' tone on her cellphone made her jump, startling her out of her crying. She pulled it out of her pocket to examine it. Having reconnected to a network, she had received a message from Pete Stillman, but it wasn't his text – *Where the hell are you?* –that had her staring at her screen, mouth agape and eyes wide. It was the date and time. Saturday 10th November, 16:47. She had been inside that house for eighteen hours.

Rosie wiped her face, stood up, then limped to the huge gates of the manor. Reaching them, she was eternally grateful to find the keys still in the ignition of Scott's car. She jumped in, then adjusted the rear-view mirror to see herself. She looked awful – even worse than she felt –so just shook her head, pushed the mirror back into position, and started the car.

Rosie Hendricks wiped her eyes, then drove away, toward whatever horrors the night held in store for her.

30

Cohen & Cohen Associates, Broadway, New York City.
Saturday 10th November 2012, 8:57pm.

Ken Price stared in disbelief as the forms of a child and a man fell from the building opposite. This had been the most terrifying day of his life, with hordes of insane people killing his work colleagues and trying to do the same to him and the small band of people who had taken refuge inside the office they were defending. Now the sight of the pair plummeting to the ground was too much for him, reinforcing the horror of it all.

He and four other office workers had barricaded themselves into the conference room, trying to shield themselves from the rampaging, psychotic horde roaming the building, but the barricaded door had been under constant siege for the past half hour and had begun to show signs of weakening.

The horror had started earlier that evening. Ken had been working late on an potential new important account, and been interrupted by his friend and colleague, Jonathan Peters, who had raced into his office declaring that something crazy had been going on; that people were being killed and butchered in the streets and that it was widespread – not only throughout New York City but the world, as the news had reported it. Ken had followed Jonathan to a television in the conference room to view the events, when screaming outside the door had caught both their terrified attention. A few people had raced into the room, shouting at those inside to help them barricade the door, which they hastily did, all the while screaming at one another and asking what the hell was going on. There they had remained for the past three and a half hours, the door under siege almost the whole time.

However, as the latest attack had raged, and Ken had looked around for something else to stack against the door, he had spied the figures falling through the air, not realizing he was walking open-mouthed from his post of reinforcing the blockade.

He stared at the falling man as he grabbed the child and turned midair, his back to the ground. Ken shook his head and called out, "Oh my God!"

One of the men at the barricade screamed at him to get back into position, but it was too late. The blockade failed, and the door crashed open. The Taken swarmed into the room and butchered them all.

The Beginning

New York City.
Friday 9th November 2012, 8:31am.
As Judas Iscariot sat in his cardboard home in the alleyway, he once more found himself thinking about the woman he had bumped into on the street the day before, and the powerful dark entity that had attached itself to her.

Normally, the troubles of other humans mattered little to him. He had been through and seen enough not to want to get involved in their problems anymore, preferring to sit alone and contemplate the mistake he had made over two thousand years ago; one for which he continued to be punished. He had considered stopping and talking to the woman, to ask her if she knew she had such a malevolent force stalking her, but what would he have said? *"Excuse me, miss, but it seems a demon has attached itself to and is sucking the life force from you. Spare any change?"* She would have laughed him back into the stone age. But something about that haunting had rattled him; it wasn't the usual fare of demons fucking with humans. Part of him continued to feel he should have done something about it, that he should have tried.

He shook his head and dismissed it. The fates of humans were no longer his concern. He had suffered too much for them, and he would do so no more.

He was about to lie down and attempt to sleep – something his cursed, undying body never truly experienced – when someone stopped outside his cardboard shelter.

"It really is a wondrous world, isn't it?" a familiar voice said. "You can see why He loves it so."

175

Judas shuffled out of his box and looked up into the face of the smartly-dressed angel.

"We have a task for you, Iscariot," the angel said, smiling.

MORE FROM THE AUTHOR

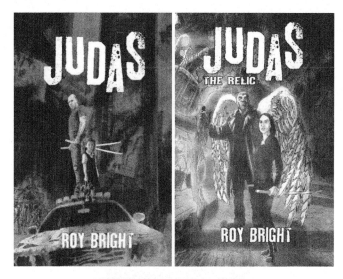

Available now from Amazon

Visit the author's website and sign up for the newsletter to be kept up to date with all future releases

www.roytbright.com

About the Author

Roy Thomas Bright was born on 22 October 1971 in Manchester U.K., and grew up in Burnley, East Lancashire.

He received his secondary education at St Wilfrid's C of E High School in Blackburn and upon leaving in 1988 decided to join the Royal Navy as a gunner. The need to patrol some of the world's 'hotspots' allowed him to travel the globe extensively, and he was very fortunate to see a vast number of exotic countries and different cultures.

In 1999 Roy decided to leave the Royal Navy to pursue a career as a professional musician. Having been a composer and arranger since the age of six and able to play a plethora of instruments, Roy went on to experience many highs in his first band Deponeye until that ended in 2004. In 2005 Roy started his second band, Exit State, which enjoyed great success touring all over the UK and parts of Europe, a No.1 video on Kerrang TV's Most Requested show, and sharing the stage with the likes of Michael Schenker of Scorpions and UFO fame, Blaze Bayley (Iron Maiden), Esoterica, Dave Evans (AC/DC), The Black Mollys, Forever Never, Black Spiders, and Neil Buchanan's Marseille.

Following a successful tour with guitar legend Michael Schenker in 2012, Exit State were delighted to be invited to become patrons of the Children's Hospice Arts charity – chART – an organization Roy is still a proud patron of today whose amazing work aims to enrich the lives of children and young people living with severe disabilities and life-limiting conditions in hospices through the creative, performing, and literary arts, enabling individual expression, creativity, and communication.

It was in late 2012 while enjoying touring downtime that Roy decided to pursue one of his other creative passions – writing. The idea for Judas had been sitting deeply within his psyche for some time and the amalgamation of the original idea fueled by the lyrics in the rock song 'What Have You Done' by Within Temptation finally saw him put pen to paper. A massive and steep learning curve followed, but he was fortunate due to connections made from his time within the music industry to receive exceptional advice from a number of sources. An introduction by Exit State's manager Mark Appleton to Stephen Clegg, the author of Maria's Papers, proved to be an invaluable one as Stephen's help and guidance was key in ensuring Judas was worthy of being published.

In 2012, Roy published Judas via Whiteley Publishing. He then re-published a 2nd edition of the novel via self-publishing in 2020 and hasn't looked back since.

Roy is thoroughly enjoying writing more and more, including screenplays with his screenwriting partner Mike Harris, and he has penned a number of original scripts, including the Judas stories.

Roy has three children: Reece, Tyler and Lily.

Printed in Great Britain
by Amazon